SINS OF THE FATHERS

SINS OF THE FATHERS

Anthea Fraser

This first world edition published 2018
in Great Britain and the USA by
SEVERN HOUSE PUBLISHERS LTD of
Eardley House, 4 Uxbridge Street, London W8 7SY.
Trade paperback edition first published
in Great Britain and the USA 2018 by
SEVERN HOUSE PUBLISHERS LTD.

British Library Cataloguing in Publication Data
A CIP catalogue record for this title is available from the British Library.

ISBN-13: 978-0-7278-8790-0 (cased)
ISBN-13: 978-1-84751-913-9 (trade paper)
ISBN-13: 978-1-78010-969-5 (e-book)

All Severn House titles are printed on acid-free paper.

Severn House Publishers support the Forest Stewardship Council™ [FSC™],
the leading international forest certification organisation.
All our titles that are printed on FSC certified paper carry the FSC logo.

Typeset by Palimpsest Book Production Ltd.,
Falkirk, Stirlingshire, Scotland.
Printed and bound in Great Britain by
TJ International, Padstow, Cornwall.

FAMILIES, FRIENDS AND ACQUAINTANCES

In Drumlee, Angus

Mark Richmond/Adam Ryder
Douglas Crawford
Paula Crawford, his wife
Sebastian Crawford, their elder son
Harry Crawford, their younger son
Helena Crawford, their elder daughter
Natalie Crawford, their younger daughter
Jessica Crawford, Harry's wife
Danny Crawford, Seb's son
Nick Pagett, Natalie's fiancé

Callum and Lexie Mackay, owners of the Merlin Hotel
Blair Mackay, their son
Ailsa Dupont, their daughter, married to Jean-Luc, the chef at
  the hotel

In Kent

Mark Richmond
Sophie Richmond, his wife
Florence Richmond, their daughter

Charles Richmond, Mark's father
Margot Richmond, Mark's mother
Jonathan Richmond, his brother
Delia Richmond, Jonathan's new wife

Peter Kingsley, Sophie's father
Lydia Kingsley, Sophie's mother

Simon Lester, Mark's colleague
Jenny Lester, Simon's wife

Stella Jordan, Sophie's friend
Lance Grenville
James Meredith

In Clapham, London

Ellie Mallory
Sybil Mallory
Tom, Ellie's boyfriend

ONE

S tanding in the centre of his sitting room, Mark Richmond went through a mental checklist. Bills paid, boiler turned off, newspapers cancelled, electric devices unplugged.

It was a stroke of luck that he'd pre-booked this early spring break, because, one way and another, he'd had about as much as he could take. And when he came back, he promised himself, he'd put the house on the market. Like a host of other things, it was now part of his past. He'd abandon it, he told himself firmly, with as little regret as a snake shedding its skin.

His eyes moved broodingly round the pleasant room with its host of memories, good and bad, and came to rest on the bookcase and the studio portrait on top of it. On impulse he walked over and, ignoring the photo, skimmed along the row of titles before deciding after all not to remove any; he'd read those that interested him and had no wish to add weight to his modest luggage. Luckily he'd done a lot of backpacking in his youth and was adept at travelling light.

Despite himself, his eyes lifted to the lovely face in its frame. Nor would he be taking *her* with him, he thought with suppressed venom, and, picking up the photo, replaced it with a satisfying thump face down.

Time to be going. Wheeling his case out of the front door, he stowed it in the boot of the car and set off for the station.

There was a queue for tickets at King's Cross and Mark glanced impatiently at his watch. His train was due to leave in twenty minutes, but as long as they kept moving he should make it in time.

He'd almost reached the window when his arm was grabbed and he was pulled forcibly to one side. 'What the—?' he began angrily, before registering to his surprise that his assailant was a young woman.

'*There* you are!' she was exclaiming. 'I'd almost given you up! What are you queuing for? I *said* I'd get the tickets! Now come on or we'll miss the train!'

He pulled back. 'There must be some mistake; we've never met—'

'I know *that*!' she said impatiently. Despite his resistance she was dragging him with her along the concourse. 'Do hurry up! I'll fill in the details once we're on the train.'

'But I've no idea—'

'I've *told* you, I'll explain.'

Whoever she was, she seemed prone to speaking in italics. They stopped at a barrier and he saw that the waiting train was bound for Aberdeen rather than York, his intended destination. But by now his curiosity was aroused: who the hell was this determined young woman, who acknowledged they'd never met, yet was set on his joining her? And how would she react when she discovered her error?

There was only one way to find out. After all, he'd nothing better to do and she seemed to have a ticket for him. His plans, such as they were, wouldn't suffer from a day's delay. Come to that, he'd not booked in anywhere, and Scotland was as good a place as Yorkshire for a walking holiday. Alternatively – and perhaps the best course – once she'd explained herself he could leave both her and the train at the first stop, which, according to the board, would be Stevenage.

'Coach B,' she was saying. 'Typical! Right at the far end!'

Her mobile chimed from the depths of her handbag but she ignored it as she made her way purposefully between throngs of hurrying fellow passengers.

'At last!' she exclaimed, coming to a halt and opening a carriage door. 'Can you stow the luggage while I find our seats?'

And, casting aside his last doubts, Mark did as she requested before following her down the length of the coach.

'Now,' he said, taking the seat beside her, 'perhaps you'll be good enough to tell me what the hell's going on?'

'Hang on a minute.' She opened her bag, took out her mobile and pressed voicemail. The voice that reached them, harried and breathless, was hard to make out against considerable background noise.

'Ms Crawford, it's David Lauder from Benton's. I'm extremely sorry, I've been held up all along the line – first traffic, then we stopped between stations on the tube and I'd no signal. I haven't a hope of making the train, but there's another in an hour or so. If you text me the address, I'll join you there. My apologies again.'

Mark's abductor spun towards him, doubt suddenly flooding her face.

'Then who the hell are *you*?' she demanded accusingly, and out on the platform the guard's whistle blew and the train began to move.

Mark leaned back, able to study her for the first time. Early thirties, at a guess. Short red-gold hair, pale skin. Not his type – too bossy, for a start.

'I might ask you the same question,' he said. 'There I was, minding my own business, when you suddenly seize hold of me and drag me on to this train.'

'Kicking and screaming? Hardly. You could have stopped me if you'd really wanted to.' Still the accusatory tone.

'I tried, but you wouldn't listen. Then curiosity got the better of me.'

She drew a deep breath. 'But I don't know anything about you,' she said.

'Likewise. Though you don't seem to know much about the guy you were supposed to meet, either.'

'At least he'd been vetted.'

Mark raised an eyebrow. '*Vetted?*'

She flushed, the colour staining her pale cheeks. 'I suppose I owe you an explanation,' she said slowly. 'David Lauder, who phoned just now, belongs to a firm I use now and then, which provides partners for business people, to attend functions and so on when required. And no,' she added quickly, as his eyebrow lifted again, 'it is *not* an escort agency, it's on a purely business basis.'

'I never doubted it,' he said gravely, and she threw him a suspicious glance.

'Well, as I needed someone for the next week or so, I contacted them. Unfortunately my usual partner wasn't free so it was arranged this David Lauder would stand in for him.

We were to meet under the clock and he was described as being tall and fair, wearing a dark blue windcheater and with a tartan wheelie case.'

'Which would fit half the male population of London.'

'So it would appear,' she said drily. 'Where were you intending to go?'

'York, on a walking holiday.'

'At least you hadn't forked out for your ticket.'

Was he supposed to be grateful? He turned the conversation back to her. 'So why is a "partner" required on this occasion, and for as long as a week?'

She hesitated. 'Perhaps before we go any further we should introduce ourselves. I'm Helena Crawford – not, if you please, Hel-*aina*, or Hel-*eena*. Accent on *Hel*, as my brothers never fail to point out.'

'Mark Richmond,' he said.

She solemnly held out her hand and he as solemnly shook it.

'So why the need for a partner?' he repeated.

'To pre-empt my sister.' She flushed again. 'Not a very worthy aim, I grant you, but I was intending to pass you – or rather David Lauder – off as my fiancé.' She looked at him challengingly. 'Are you up for that?'

'What does it entail?'

'A week's free holiday, for a start.' A smile tugged at the corner of her mouth. 'Don't worry, you wouldn't be required to sleep with me! You'd be standing in for David, so the Benton's rules apply. In any case I'll be sharing with my sister – we often have to on these occasions.'

'And what *is* the occasion?'

'My parents' ruby wedding anniversary. And, if I'm not mistaken, the announcement of my sister's engagement. Hence the need to get in first, so to speak.'

'It seems a bit pointless, if you don't mind my saying so. You'll be found out sooner rather than later.'

'Oh, after a week or two I'll say I'd dumped you. It wouldn't be a problem – none of us live near each other. So what do you think? Are you still going to pull the communication cord?'

He smiled reluctantly. 'Let's say I'm intrigued. But tell me more. For a start, who's involved in this celebration?'

'My mother and father, of course – Paula and Douglas Crawford; my brother Sebastian; my other brother Harry and his wife Jessica; and my sister Natalie with her soon-to-be fiancé, one Nick Pagett. And, of course, us – they know I'm bringing someone. Making nine in all. It'll be a bit of a squeeze and I'm afraid you'd be sharing with the unknown Nick.'

'Even so, it's a hefty bill for your parents.'

'Oh, it's not a hotel, it's our second home. I haven't been for a while, but when we were children we spent all our holidays there.' She gave a mock shiver. 'Though God knows what it's like this early in the year. Scotland in February! Blame the parents – what a month to get married! On Valentine's Day, would you believe!'

Mark was silent, turning things over in his mind before saying, 'And it's in Aberdeen?'

'No, we get off at Montrose, which is the nearest station. Then it's a good half hour's drive to Drumlee. Seb will meet us.'

'What time are we due to arrive?'

'About five, I think.'

He looked at his watch and gave a low whistle. 'That's a hell of a journey! Why in heaven's name don't you fly?'

'Because, though I hate to admit it, I'm a wimp. I had a nightmare experience when I was little, and it put me right off.'

He glanced out of the window at the rapidly passing suburbs. 'And to get this straight, at the end of a week we go our separate ways? No strings of any kind?'

'Positively none. One of Benton's strictest rules.'

Not that they applied in his case, but he couldn't imagine wanting to prolong the charade. As she'd said, it was only for a week, and since he'd booked a fortnight's leave he could still go walking at the end of it.

She turned to look at him. Her eyes were her best feature, large, dark-lashed and periwinkle-blue. 'So what do you think? If you're prepared to go ahead I'll have to text David and stop him coming.'

His decision, he found, was already made. 'I'm game if you are,' he said.

*   *   *

As the journey progressed they exchanged as much information as she considered necessary for the role to be played.

'You'll be interested to hear we've had a whirlwind romance,' she ended with a smile. 'I told the family we've only known each other about six weeks and purposely avoided going into details. I had to give you a name, though, so I chose Adam Ryder. Apart from that, you're free just to be yourself,' she added, with a satisfaction he didn't share.

She turned to him suddenly as a thought struck her. 'God, I haven't asked if you're married! I sort of assumed, since you're on your own . . .' Her voice tailed off uncertainly.

'In a manner of speaking, I am,' he replied.

She frowned. 'What does that mean?'

'My wife's not around at the moment.'

'Children?'

'A four-year-old daughter.' His heart twisted at the thought of Florence.

'Also not around?'

'Correct.'

A lopsided smile. 'With that baggage, I doubt if you'd qualify for Benton's!'

'I'll bear that in mind when I'm job-hunting.'

She raised an eyebrow. '*Are* you job-hunting?'

'Not actively.'

She gave an exclamation of impatience. 'Not very forthcoming, are you?'

She didn't know the half of it. 'No reason why I should be.'

'True,' she conceded after a moment, and asked no further questions.

By the time the train finally pulled into Montrose station Mark was already having second thoughts. Tired as he was after the journey and the succession of sleepless nights that had preceded it, he was far from sure he'd be convincing as the would-be husband of the young woman he'd just met. *Adam Ryder*, he reminded himself, wryly acknowledging that it'd be a relief to escape Mark Richmond, albeit temporarily.

What would Sophie have made of all this? he wondered with grim amusement as he stepped down on to the platform. But thoughts of Sophie, like all else he'd left behind, were strictly taboo and he hastily stifled them.

In this he was helped by an excited cry of 'Auntie Helena!', followed by the approach at speed of a small boy who hurled himself at Mark's companion and wound his arms round her legs.

'Danny!' she exclaimed laughingly. 'Careful – you'll trip me up! What are you doing here?'

A tall man in a Barbour jacket joined them, his collar turned up against the cold wind that swept down the platform. This, Mark recalled from Helena's summary, must be the divorced brother.

'The whole family's invited,' he remarked, bending to kiss his sister's cheek, 'and as luck would have it, it's half-term next week.'

He turned to Mark, holding out his hand. 'Sebastian Crawford.'

'Oh, sorry!' Helena broke in. 'Seb, this is—'

'Adam Ryder,' Mark said smoothly, taking the extended hand. 'How do you do?'

Sebastian nodded, his eyes briefly raking Mark's face. Then he turned back to Helena and relieved her of her case. 'Right, let's get going. The car's just outside.'

The drop in temperature was traumatic after the warmth of the train, but as they reached the car park his key set lights flashing on a grey BMW a few yards ahead of them and, as Danny was insisting Helena join him in the back, Mark settled gratefully into the warm passenger seat.

'A heavy frost's forecast for tonight,' Sebastian remarked, sliding in beside him, 'but with luck we'll escape it on the coast.'

'Has everyone else arrived?' Helena asked from the back seat.

'Yep; the parents have been here a few days, organizing things. Danny and I flew up this afternoon with Harry and Jess, then waited at the airport till Nat and Nick's plane landed, to save Dad a double journey.'

'What's he like, this Nick?' Helena enquired curiously.

'Seems a decent guy. Fellow medic.'

Mark had learned from her brief outline that Helena's sister was a GP, one of her brothers a solicitor and the other in civil engineering, but his tired brain couldn't recall which was which. He leaned back against the headrest and closed his eyes, letting the exchange of family gossip wash over him. The warmth of the car, the gentle rhythm of its passage and the low hum of conversation combined to lull him into semi-consciousness, and the complications of his life, temporarily displaced by the unexpected turn of events, flooded back into his brain.

Who had he been fooling? he thought wearily. All right, so he'd escaped for the moment but eventually he'd have to go back to find the same problems awaiting him. God, how had he got himself into this mess? If this was what came of doing a good turn, he'd make damn sure he never did another.

He must have dropped off, because the next thing he was aware of was the cessation of movement, and he jerked awake to find the car at a standstill outside a solid stone house.

The front door was immediately flung open and a woman stood outlined against a background of light. Struggling back to consciousness, Mark fumbled clumsily with his seatbelt, wincing at the draught of freezing air as Sebastian got out and opened the boot to retrieve their luggage. Then, having claimed his own case, he followed Helena and Danny up the steps to the open doorway, where Helena was enfolded in a warm embrace.

'And this is Adam, Mum,' she said, extricating herself, and Mrs Crawford turned smilingly to him.

'Welcome, Adam! Perhaps I may hug you too, to welcome you into the family?' And, feeling a fraud, Mark submitted to her embrace, mumbling what he hoped was an appropriate response.

The hall suddenly filled with people converging from all directions to welcome Helena and her new fiancé, and his sleep-numbed brain struggled hopelessly to register their names.

'Come and get warm!' Mrs Crawford instructed, and led him into a brightly lit room where, he was thankful to see, a log fire roared in the grate. 'And this is my husband,' she added, as a tall, grey-haired man came forward and held out his hand.

'Douglas Crawford,' he said. 'Adam, isn't it? Welcome to the clan! Can I offer you a dram to dispel the cold?'

'Thank you, that would be great.'

What he really wanted was a long, hot shower, but there seemed little prospect of one at the moment. He looked round for Helena, but she was engaged in fielding questions from members of her family.

'No, we've not chosen the ring yet,' he heard her say. 'I'm being very choosy and we're still looking.'

Douglas Crawford returned with a glass filled with golden liquid. 'This'll warm the cockles!' he said. 'Now, if you'll excuse me, I'll leave Nick here to look after you while I go and greet my daughter.'

As he moved away a man Mark had glimpsed briefly in the hall took his place. Tall and lanky, he had dark wavy hair and wore glasses. At a guess, he was a few years Mark's junior.

'A bit overwhelming, isn't it?' he said with a sympathetic grin, holding out his hand. 'Nick Pagett. I went through this myself a couple of hours ago, and Nat and I aren't even engaged yet!'

Mark smiled back. '"Yet" being the operative word, I gather?'

'We don't want to steal our hosts' thunder, but I gather it's an open secret.'

'Congratulations!'

'Likewise!'

Mrs Crawford, mindful of her hostess duties, detached herself from the group round her daughter and came to join them. 'Supper will be in half an hour,' she said. 'Adam, I'm sure you'd like to freshen up; perhaps, Nick, you'd take him to your room? I do apologize for your having to share when you don't even know each other, but accommodation is somewhat limited.'

'It'll be fine,' Nick assured her, and the two men left the

room. Now that the hall was empty of people, Mark saw that it was large and square and, after the warmth of the sitting room, decidedly cool despite two old-fashioned radiators against the wall.

Intercepting his glance, Nick said, 'I hope you've brought your thermals! Nat apologized for the temperature; they're usually here in summer, of course.'

An open doorway opposite showed a long table laid for dinner. Though the room was in darkness, flickering firelight promised an additional heat source. Retrieving his case, Mark followed Nick up the steep staircase. The upstairs landing was also large and square, and the stairs continued to another floor.

'Sebastian and the little boy are sleeping up there,' Nick said. 'And this is us,' he added as he opened the second door on the right and switched on the light. It was a pleasant room, though the pale blue walls gave rise to an instinctive shiver on this February evening. The twin beds, Mark noted with vague relief, were on opposite sides of the room, with the window between them. There was a large, old-fashioned wardrobe, a dressing table, two upright chairs and, in one corner, a washbasin with two towels hanging on a rail.

'The shower room and loo is next door,' Nick told him, 'and there's also a family-sized bathroom. Mr and Mrs Crawford have an en suite, which I'm told they installed some years ago, but for anything other than a quick sluice the rest of us will have to queue.'

'A quick sluice will do fine for now,' Mark said. 'I'm pretty shattered after the journey and hopefully it'll wake me up a bit.'

'Yes, I was surprised to hear you were coming by train. It must have been a hell of a slog.'

There was a holdall on the far bed and a library book on the table beside it. Nick Pagett said quickly, 'The beds look identical, but if you have any preference . . .?'

'No, no, none at all.' Mark lifted his own case on to the nearer one and unzipped it. Little had he thought, when packing that morning, that he would be opening it in Scotland at the home of a pseudo-fiancée!

'I'll leave you to unpack, then,' Nick said. 'There's plenty of room in the wardrobe and the two bottom drawers of the dressing table are empty. Come down when you're ready.'

He went out, closing the door behind him. Mark drew a deep breath and, taking his mobile out of his pocket, switched it off and put it in one of the allotted drawers. The next few days would be complicated enough without any rogue calls from the office and he was, after all, on holiday. Then, shrugging off his jacket, he went to the basin and turned the hot tap full on.

Paula Crawford turned as her husband came into the kitchen carrying a tray of dirty glasses.

'Well, what do you think of him?' she demanded.

'Adam? A bit reticent, but he was probably overwhelmed by a superfluity of Crawfords, poor chap.'

'He doesn't seem at all Helena's type,' Paula said worriedly, 'whereas Nick's obviously perfect for Natalie. You can tell that just by looking at them.'

'I'm not sure we know what Helena's type *is*,' Douglas returned mildly.

'Well, they've only known each other five minutes, and he's certainly very different from Jack.'

'For which, after all that trauma, we should be sincerely thankful.' He patted her shoulder as she lifted a casserole out of the oven. 'You worry too much, my dear. The only thing concerning me is that we'll have to fork out for two weddings within a few months of each other!'

Paula turned to look at him. 'And that's *really* the only thing concerning you?' she asked, her eyes raking his face.

'Now don't start that up again,' Douglas said briskly. 'We're here on a week's holiday with the family, and I intend to enjoy every minute of it.'

The evening meal was served in the dining room, and a log fire provided a welcome boost to the ancient heating system. Paula and Douglas Crawford sat at either end of the table. Mark was seated on Paula's right with Helena next to him, and Sebastian and little Danny made up the number on their side. Across from them were Nick, Natalie, Harry and Jessica.

The main course was venison casserole with a choice of vegetables, accompanied by an exceptionally good burgundy. Everyone seemed hungry and conversation was limited for the first ten minutes, during which Mark surreptitiously studied the four people opposite. It was Natalie who most interested him, and he tried without success to detect a resemblance to her sister. She was fairer than Helena, her hair hanging in a chin-length bob that framed her rather serious face, and her eyes were grey instead of blue. He'd been told she was a GP, and despite their shared medical interest she seemed an odd choice for the cheerful, outgoing Nick.

In fact it was Harry who, of all the siblings, most resembled Helena, with his coppery hair and vivid blue eyes. His wife Jessica, seated next to him, was a pale girl with shoulder-length hair and a sulky expression, who had barely spoken. It might have been his imagination, but Mark thought he'd detected an atmosphere between them; he'd noticed that Harry kept trying without success to draw her into the conversation, and wondered humorously if he'd blotted his copybook and was attempting to make amends.

Paula turned to him, interrupting his musings. 'Well, Adam,' she said smilingly, 'though we'd not met either you or Nick before, we'd already heard quite a bit about him from Natalie, whereas you are something of an unknown quantity! So do enlighten us! Do you live in London?'

Helena's foot nudged his warningly.

'I work there,' Mark answered cautiously, 'but I actually live in Chislehurst.'

'So what's your line of work?'

You're free to be yourself, she'd said, and, having heard that when embarked on a lie it was as well to keep to the truth as far as possible, he complied.

'I'm a Fine Arts valuer.'

Douglas, at the far end of the table, leaned forward. 'How very interesting! I've always wondered—'

But what he wondered they never learned, for Danny's treble voice interrupted him. Mark had almost forgotten the child, since he'd been very quiet and was not in his line of sight.

'Please can I go to bed now, Daddy?' he was asking plaintively.

There was sympathetic laughter and Paula exclaimed, 'Oh, darling, I'm so sorry – we've been too busy talking. It *is* late, but surely you'd like some pudding if I get it now?'

Danny shook his head, knuckling his eyes, and Sebastian got to his feet. 'Then bed it is, kiddo. Kiss Granny and Grandpa goodnight and I'll take you up.'

The little boy did so and he and Sebastian left the room. Paula stood up and, helped by her daughters, cleared the table and carried the dishes through to the kitchen, returning minutes later with the dessert and a cheese board.

She smiled at Mark and Nick. 'I hope you boys like trifle!' she said. 'It's a family tradition that we have it on our first night here.'

To Mark's relief the interruption had diverted attention and the resumed conversation was more general.

'Have you touched base yet with the Mackays?' Harry asked.

'Yes, we had dinner there the day we arrived.' Paula turned to the newcomers. 'They're the family who own the Merlin Hotel. We used to stay there before we bought this house and we became friends, the children playing together and so on. They're all much of an age: Blair comes between Seb and Harry, and Ailsa between Helena and Nat.'

'But the connection goes back still further,' put in Douglas with a smile. 'Paula and I met while on holiday at the hotel, back in the dark ages! It was run by Callum's parents then.'

'Are Blair and Ailsa still around?' Natalie enquired.

'Indeed, yes.' It was Paula who replied. 'Blair's helping to run the hotel and Ailsa's married to the French chef.'

'One way of holding on to him!' Harry remarked jokingly.

'And of course we'll be there for our anniversary dinner.'

'Is Blair married?' Natalie asked idly, glancing at Helena as she speared a piece of Stilton.

'No; still the most eligible bachelor in town!'

'And no doubt still playing the field,' Sebastian said drily. He'd caught the tail end of the conversation as he returned after settling his son. Jessica passed him the cheese board, which he accepted with a nod of thanks.

Mark's eyes went from one speaker to another, still hoping
to form impressions of this family into which he'd been so
unexpectedly thrust. Though conversation had flowed freely
he'd been vaguely aware of underlying tension, but unable to
pin down its source. Possibly there was more than one.

Belatedly aware that he should make some contribution, he
thanked Paula for the meal.

'I'm glad you enjoyed it, but I can't claim any credit,' she
told him. 'As it's my holiday too, a local couple comes in to
cook the evening meal and wash up afterwards. Regarding
lunch, though, which we're never in for in the summer, I
suggest it should be self-service as and when required. There's
plenty of eggs, bacon, soup and so on. Is everyone happy
with that?'

There was general agreement, and she pushed her chair
back from the table. 'Then if everyone's finished, let's go back
to the sitting room so Meg and Andy can clear away.'

'God, it's cold!' Helena exclaimed a couple of hours later.
She stood in the centre of the bedroom, clutching an empty
hot water bottle to her chest.

'At least they brought extra blankets with them,' Natalie said,
'but Mum thought it wasn't worth investing in electric ones,
as we're not likely to be here again at this time of year.'

'For which heaven be praised!'

'Give me your hottie and I'll fill it with mine before one
of the boys nabs the bathroom. It's too fiddly trying to do it
at the basin.'

'Thanks.' Helena looked disparagingly about her. 'I'd
forgotten how primitive it is,' she said plaintively.

'Well, we'll just have to make the best of it and be thankful
for the fan heater.'

By the time she returned Helena was in her dressing gown,
brushing her teeth at the basin.

'So: you're engaged!' she commented, dropping one of the
filled bottles on her sister's bed.

Helena turned from the basin. 'By which you mean wonders
never cease!'

'Seriously, Hellie, are you sure this isn't on the rebound?'

'Of course I'm sure.' She met Natalie's eyes challengingly. 'Why? Don't you like him?'

'I've barely spoken to him, but he did seem rather . . . reserved.'

'Faced with the lot of us, can you blame him?'

'No, but—'

'Jack would have turned on the charm?' Helena finished for her.

Natalie flushed. 'Sorry, that's not what I meant.'

'Be honest – yes, it was. But Jack, as I finally discovered to my cost, was all on the surface. There's more . . . depth . . . to Adam.' Helena paused. 'I liked your Nick.'

Natalie's face brightened. 'Did you? I can't quite believe how happy I am!'

'Par for the course, I'm told. When are you going to announce the engagement?'

'On Wednesday probably, so as not to detract from Mum and Dad's celebrations.'

'Champagne two nights running!' Helena said lightly.

But later, awake in the dark, the reservations that had been lying in wait till she'd nothing to distract her descended in force. Who *was* this man she'd so carelessly introduced into her family? She knew nothing whatever about him. God, she'd even forgotten his real name! While she had, perforce, supplied him with a wealth of personal detail, all he'd volunteered was that he was married 'in a manner of speaking' and had a four-year-old daughter!

So where *were* they, if they were 'not around at the moment'? For all she knew, he could have buried them under the patio! She moved her head impatiently on the pillow. That, of course, was ridiculous, but a more realistic worry was that she wasn't even sure she liked him. How could she spend the next seven days pretending to be in love, and how would he in turn indicate that he loved her?

Jack! The thought of him was a physical pain. She'd been so *sure* of him, so confident that they'd be together the rest of their lives. She still didn't know what had gone wrong, exactly when or why he'd stopped loving her. The family must think her very shallow to have fallen in love again so soon;

even pretending to have done so tarnished the memory. So what in the name of heaven had possessed her to embark on this childish charade? To her shame she knew the answer: her determination not to let her sister beat her to the altar. Yet as 'Adam' had said, its effect could only be temporary, so it was pointless anyway.

Oh God, if only she could turn the clock back! But the stark fact was that having instigated this farce she would have to see it through, or risk further humiliation. Stoically she turned on her side and willed sleep to come.

Across the landing Mark was also awake. He'd been hoping for a talk with Helena that evening; they'd not spoken privately since their arrival and he was badly in need of guidance. For instance, when and where was this whirlwind romance of theirs supposed to have started? It was as well this hadn't been Paula's first question. And although Helena had told her family nothing about him, she would obviously have told *him* about *them*. What was he supposed to know? The name of Sebastian's estranged wife? How long Harry and Jessica had been married?

But the opportunity hadn't arisen and, since they'd all had tiring journeys, an early night had been suggested and he'd found himself preparing for bed still very unsure of the role he was expected to play. He could only hope things would look clearer after a good night's sleep.

But though he was physically exhausted, as soon as the light was out his brain went into overdrive, and try as he might he couldn't deactivate it. All the problems he'd been hoping to escape flooded into his head, compounded by this new set of complications. How the *hell* had he become involved with Helena Crawford? Why hadn't he at least stuck to his plan to leave the train at Stevenage? Had he done so, he would now be comfortably settled in some centrally heated B&B with the pleasant prospect of long walks ahead of him, during which he could work out how to repair the train wreck his life had become.

For train wreck it undoubtedly was – a succession of disasters, starting with the state of his marriage. He and Sophie had known each other all their lives and their families, being friends, had tacitly assumed they'd come together. So, when no serious contenders appeared on either side, they had dutifully done so, drifting into marriage to the satisfaction of both families, if not entirely to their own – hardly a basis for stability. And after five years of increasing incompatibility the point of no return had now been reached. It was, he accepted, only their daughter who'd kept them together this long.

Then, in addition to this ongoing worry, a crisis had developed at work – arising, ironically enough, out of an agreement to help a colleague, which had swiftly boomeranged and was in danger of damaging his career.

Finally, and by far the most traumatically, there was his father and . . . But here his mind clamped down, refusing even to contemplate it.

It was another forty-five minutes before he finally fell asleep to the sound of Nick's gently rhythmic snores.

TWO

Having narrowly missed his usual train, Mark was not in the best of moods as he fought his way on to the next one. There'd been a series of problems at work which, his PA having gone home with a migraine, he'd had to deal with himself, but the main cause of his discomfort – and, he imagined, that of his fellow travellers – was London itself, unbearable in this prolonged heatwave with its baking pavements and clogged, fume-filled air. And to crown it all, he reflected sourly, unlike the rest of the country's workforce, he was not looking forward to the weekend.

Naturally there were no seats and he was forced to straphang, swaying precariously as the train lurched forward and unable either to check his emails or read the evening paper. Par for the course, he told himself, fixing his thoughts on a cold drink and a shower as soon as he reached home.

Sophie and Florence, he remembered, were going to tea with Sophie's friend Stella and her precocious child, neither of whom he cared for, which meant Florence would be over-excited and Sophie would have either seen or been told about Stella's latest acquisition, and try to persuade him to buy one. And if he protested that they'd no need of it, she'd simply shrug and say lightly, 'Never mind, if it's too expensive Daddy will get it for us.'

Couldn't she *see* how that infuriated him? He'd known her father for as long as she had – he'd been 'Uncle Peter' throughout Mark's childhood – but fond though he was of his father-in-law, he was profoundly irritated by his inability to refuse his daughter anything, and was determined that Florence wouldn't grow up expecting all she desired to be handed to her on a plate.

Which, he thought with a sigh, would have been easier if

she'd had a brother or sister to share with. But her own birth had been traumatic and after a long and difficult labour Sophie, pale and exhausted, had made him promise not to put her through it again. He recalled gazing down at the small miracle that was his daughter nestling in the crook of her mother's arm and, overwhelmed by love coupled with guilt at his wife's suffering, he'd unhesitatingly done so. Later he'd assumed that, since both the request and his compliance had taken place during the emotional aftermath, neither would be considered binding; but when, after a couple of years, he'd suggested they try for another baby, Sophie's reaction had been swift and emphatic.

'No way! I'm not going through that again!' she'd declared forcefully. 'You *promised*!'

'But the second baby's always easier,' he'd protested, recalling overheard wisdom. 'It wouldn't be like last time.'

'Then *you* have it!' she'd retorted, effectively putting an end to the discussion.

He was jerked from his reflections as the train reached his stop and, joining the mass exodus, he made his way to the car park, where his car had spent ten hours in unremitting sunshine. Having burned his hand on the door, he had to wait several minutes before he could bear to get into it and drive the couple of miles home.

It was Florence's task to open the gates for him each evening, and at the sound of his approach her little face appeared at a window. Minutes later she came running out to greet him in her Pingu pyjamas and his tiredness fell away as he bent to hug her.

'You're late, Daddy!' she scolded. 'You promised to give me my bath!'

'I know, poppet, I'm sorry. I missed my train.'

She dragged the gates shut, then, taking his hand, led him into the house. 'We went to Rosie's for tea and she has a paddling pool in the garden and we splashed each other but Rosie's mummy was cross when she splashed Tobias because he didn't like it!' she said all in one breath.

Tobias, Mark recalled, was Stella's dog. 'I don't suppose he did,' he said.

Sophie came to kiss his cheek, wrinkling her nose. 'Ugh, you're all hot and sticky!'

'So would you be, after the day I've had! Sorry I'm late. Have I time for a shower before dinner?'

'Yes, it's only salad. Oh, and Stephanie's all right for tomorrow.'

Their neighbour's teenage daughter was their regular babysitter.

He frowned. 'Tomorrow?'

'Oh, Mark, you can't have forgotten! Daddy's sixtieth!'

'Of course!' His heart sank; he didn't enjoy parties at the best of times, and there'd be no one of their generation apart from Jon and his new wife, about whom he still had reservations. And it meant having to dress at least semi-formally and trailing down to Foxbridge, when all he wanted was to slob out at home.

'I put out the card for you, but you still haven't signed it,' she reminded him as he started up the stairs.

'I'll do it when I come down. Is there a bottle of wine in the fridge?'

'Yes, the Saumur.'

'Excellent. I shan't be long.'

'Then you'll read to me, won't you, Daddy?' Florence called after him.

'Of course. Go and choose which story you'd like.'

Under the cool, revitalizing shower, Mark tried to analyse the vague dissatisfaction that was now his norm. There was no obvious reason for it; although today had been a nightmare, he enjoyed his work in the Fine Arts department of a well-known auction house. No money or health worries, and he had the added bonus of a beautiful wife and daughter. So why the lack of enthusiasm for a weekend at home?

He sighed, finally admitting the answer: because, underlying all that surface wellbeing, their marriage was in a parlous state, and if he wished to save it – and he assured himself that he did – immediate steps would have to be taken.

Thoughtfully he began to soap himself, making a mental list of their individual pros and cons. For his part, he was satisfied that he'd been a good husband and father, never for an instant looking elsewhere and adoring his daughter from the moment of birth. As for his interests, they were fairly broad, encompassing the arts, obviously, in all their forms, but also taking in politics, sport and current affairs, enjoying nothing more than a vigorous debate on a wide range of subjects. On the negative side, he was impatient and frequently dismissive of other people's viewpoints.

As for Sophie, they'd first made love when he was eighteen and she sixteen, and it was the one area in their lives that was still totally satisfying. Also on the plus side, she was not only beautiful but an excellent hostess, a superb cook and a devoted mother. However, as he'd learned the hard way, she expected always to have her own way and seldom had a serious thought in her head. He doubted if she even knew or cared who was the Prime Minister, and if he tried to discuss some burning issue of the day she'd dismiss it with a wave of the hand and turn the conversation to something more trivial.

There was a knock on the bathroom door and a little voice called, 'I've chosen a story, Daddy!'

'Shan't be a minute!' he called back, and resolved both to make a more positive attempt to revive his marriage and to curb his own impatience.

This resolution was put to the test over dinner a couple of hours later, when Sophie remarked casually, 'Stella's taking Rosie to their flat in Bournemouth for a week at the end of the month, and suggested Florence and I join them.'

He put down his spoon. 'Surely that's the week before she starts "big school"?'

'Mm.' Sophie licked her own spoon.

'But I told you I'd arranged to take that week off work, so we could have some family time.'

'Did you? I don't remember. But she'd love a week at the seaside with Rosie.'

Mark tried to hold on to his temper. 'Sophie, she's been with you every day of the summer holidays, but this is my last chance to spend time with her before she becomes a fully fledged schoolgirl. I've been looking forward to it.'

'Well I'm sorry, but I've told Stella we'll go.'

'Then you can tell her you've changed your mind – that I'd made other arrangements – anything you damn well like, as long as you make it clear you're not going!'

She raised a lazy eyebrow. 'No need to shout, darling.'

'I'm not shouting!' he retorted, knowing that he was.

'We can let Florence choose,' she said peaceably.

And she'd make sure it was a loaded question, he thought angrily, gilded with mention of iced lollies and shrimping nets.

He forced himself to calm down. 'We'll have a day at the zoo and we can go to that theme park she keeps talking about. And the local cinema's running a series of Disney films. If we go to a matinée we can have an early supper at that pizza place afterwards, make it a special treat.'

Sophie sighed and began to clear the table, and the subject was dropped without any satisfactory solution being reached.

The rest of the evening passed with a minimum of conversation, Sophie seemingly enthralled by what he considered an exceptionally bland serial on TV. It wasn't until they were in bed that she played her hand, turning to face him and tracing a finger round his mouth.

'You're not really cross with me, are you, sweetie?' she wheedled.

'Yes, I am,' he replied, but without conviction.

'I didn't mean to upset you,' she said contritely. 'I'd forgotten you'd arranged time off work. Can you swap the week for half-term or something?'

He meant to stick to his guns; in truth, he'd been dreading this milestone in his daughter's life. Would she be happy, after the informality of nursery school? Would the other children bully her? Would she still be the sweet and innocent child she was now?

He began to formulate these arguments, but Sophie's fingers were moving inexorably downwards and with a groan he abandoned them and pulled her into his arms.

The Kingsleys lived in the village of Foxbridge on the outskirts of Sevenoaks, and as Mark turned into the lane they could see a long line of parked cars. Swearing under his breath, he drew in behind them.

'I told you we should have left earlier,' Sophie complained. 'We're probably the last to arrive.'

'In which case, my love, you can make an entrance!' he said facetiously. Then added, at her suspicious glance, 'And believe me, you'll be worth the wait!'

With a fleeting smile, she set off along the uneven pavement in her high-heeled sandals and, after collecting their gift from the boot, Mark followed her. The day was even hotter than the previous one and, bereft of the car's air-con, he was already uncomfortable. A long, cool Pimm's, a staple of the Kingsleys' summer entertaining, would go down a treat, he thought; thank God Sophie, who did not need alcohol to make her sparkle, would be driving home.

For as long as he could remember, Mark had considered Dormers his ideal house, despite his father's sardonic allusions to 'Kingsley Castle'. It was built in the style of a traditional oast house with the roundel, a cone-topped tower in rust-coloured brick, at one end, while the rest of the house was fronted in white weatherboard under a red-tiled roof. In the flush of first love he'd imagined Sophie, who at the time had had long hair, leaning out of a window in the tower like a modern-day Rapunzel.

Now, skirting another four cars, he followed her up the wide gravelled drive and round the side of the house to the extensive back garden, where some two dozen people with glasses in their hands stood talking and laughing. Uniformed staff moved among them with trays of drinks and a marquee had been set up with tables laid for lunch. Outside caterers, Mark noted; another target for his father's barbed comments.

It was Lydia Kingsley, Sophie's mother, who saw them first and came hurrying to welcome them. 'There you are!' she exclaimed. 'Did you run into heavy traffic?'

'No,' Sophie answered, 'we were late leaving.'

'Well, you're here now.' She kissed her daughter's cheek, then Mark's, nodding at the package in his hand. 'If you'll give me that, Mark, I'll put it with the other gifts in the conservatory to open later. Now, let's find you both a drink. Most people are opting for Pimm's.'

'Sounds perfect,' Sophie said.

Seeing the two women together, Mark was again struck by their similarity, both small and blonde with identical smiles. Lydia, though in her late fifties, could almost be taken for her daughter's contemporary, with her smooth skin and trim figure. He'd never seen her other than perfectly groomed and beautifully (for which read expensively) dressed, today in sea-green silk. But, like Sophie, she had never in his hearing discussed anything more profound than a new recipe or their latest holiday. Which made his own mother's friendship with her all the more perplexing, since Margot Richmond was a strong-minded, opinionated woman who didn't suffer fools gladly.

'Mark!'

He turned as his brother Jonathan bore down on him, followed by his wife. 'Thank God you're here! I was beginning to think you'd flunked it and there'd be no one under fifty to talk to!'

'Well, you can relax; salvation is at hand.'

'Where's Soph?' Having known her since babyhood, Jonathan persisted with the nickname, to Sophie's continuing annoyance.

'Getting a Pimm's,' Mark replied. He nodded at his sister-in-law. 'Delia.'

She nodded back. She was, Mark thought, very dramatic looking – at just under six foot the same height as Jonathan, with a heavy black fringe and very blue eyes. They'd made a striking pair at their wedding a couple of months previously, but there was something about her that made him uneasy, though he couldn't have said what it was.

Jonathan leaned forward, lowering his voice. 'Between you and me, old Peter's been knocking it back a bit.'

Mark raised an eyebrow. 'Well, it is his birthday. He's entitled to let his hair down.'

Sophie's return with two glasses of Pimm's put an end to the exchange.

'Soph, my love!' Jonathan greeted her. 'As gorgeous as ever!'

She submitted to his peck and smiled at Delia before turning to Mark and handing him one of the glasses. 'Let's go and find Daddy and wish him happy birthday.'

Peter Kingsley wasn't hard to locate. As they moved into the throng of people his laugh rang out loudly and, catching sight of them, he held his arms wide, spilling some of his drink on to the grass.

'Here they are at last!' he cried. 'My beautiful daughter and my favourite son-in-law!'

Jon had been right, Mark thought uneasily as he submitted to the bear hug. The party had hardly begun but their host seemed several drinks ahead of the rest of them. Well, as he'd pointed out, it *was* his birthday. Nevertheless, in all the years he'd known him Mark had never seen Peter Kingsley the worse for drink, and Sophie's fleeting frown showed she shared his disquiet.

'Isn't it a glorious day?' Peter was exclaiming – too loudly. 'Lyddie was afraid the weather would break, but I knew it would hold for us, and all my wonderful friends have come to join in the celebration!'

An expansive gesture encompassed those nearest to him who, Mark thought, looked slightly uncomfortable. He recognized several of them, long-standing friends of his parents as well as the Kingsleys, and was wondering how to respond when he saw with relief that his father was approaching. If anyone could handle Peter in his cups, it would be Charles Richmond. The two men had met at university, been each other's best man and joined the same firm of chartered accountants. Charles's often caustic comments about his friend were, Mark was sure, a sign of his underlying affection.

Having greeted his son and daughter-in-law, Charles put a hand on Peter's arm. 'Lydia has sent me to usher you all into the marquee. Lunch is about to be served.'

Which, Mark thought thankfully, joining in the general move, might well solve the problem.

Unfortunately, it didn't. Mark and Sophie were seated at a table for six with Jonathan and Delia and a partner from the accountancy firm and his wife, who introduced themselves as

Michael and Sarah. They were some way from the top table, but throughout the meal of watercress soup, chicken in aspic and raspberry ice-cream cake Peter's laugh continually rang out, and at one point, a minor disturbance involving waiters with napkins indicated that he'd overturned his neighbour's wine glass.

Sophie had lost her sparkle, and Mark noticed with a tug of the heart that her eyes kept straying anxiously in her father's direction. He reached under the table to squeeze her hand, and was rewarded by a brief smile.

The climax for which he'd been mentally preparing himself came with the advent of the birthday cake. It was conveyed to the top table with some ceremony and a spontaneous round of applause, a glorious confection on a silver stand. The obligatory song was sung, Peter – after several attempts – blew out the token six candles, and then came the cries of 'Speech! Speech!'

Mark held his breath as their host stumbled to his feet again and stood, swaying slightly and beaming jovially around. Lydia was looking up at him anxiously, biting her lip, and Mark felt Sophie stiffen at his side.

'I'd just like to thank you all for coming,' he began, his voice slurred. 'I've had a wonderful life, and would like to thank my lovely wife for all the love and support she's given me—'

He half-turned towards Lydia, lost his balance and stumbled forward, landing on the cake and sending it crashing to the ground in a snowstorm of shattered icing. There was a brief, stunned silence while he stood looking at the destruction in almost comical dismay. Then Charles rose quickly and took his arm. 'Not feeling too good, old chap?' he asked solicitously. 'It's very hot in here – let's get you some air.' And with a hand under Peter's elbow he walked him quickly out of the tent, followed by Lydia, murmuring a general distressed, 'Excuse us!'

Sophie burst into tears and ran after them and Mark, hesitating a moment, flung a look of apology at the horrified faces around him before following her. He caught up with her on the terrace and, grabbing her arm, pulled her round to face him.

'No, sweetheart, let them go,' he urged as, still sobbing, she struggled to free herself. 'Dad and your mum can deal with it. He wouldn't want you to see him in that state.'

'He's ill!' she cried. 'He must be! I've never seen him like this before!'

'I know, love. Everyone will have been drinking his health and he'll have felt he had to respond, no doubt on an empty stomach.'

She shook her head, unconvinced. Mark glanced back across the garden. Through the marquee opening he could see that subdued conversation had resumed and wondered what he should do. As a family member perhaps he ought to go back and apologize, but he couldn't leave Sophie in this distressed state. It was with a wave of relief that he heard his mother's voice rise above the others. Good old Mum! She'd see to things.

He turned back to Sophie and led her through the conservatory, past the table piled with gaily wrapped packages, into the cool of the hall. There was no sign of the other three; he assumed they'd gone upstairs. He was about to turn into the sitting room when a member of the catering staff appeared in the kitchen doorway, looking worried.

'Would it be in order to serve coffee now, sir?' he enquired.

That would ease matters, Mark reflected thankfully. 'Good idea,' he said. 'Unfortunately there was an accident with the cake, so it would be great if someone could go down and clear it up. As you probably saw, Mr Kingsley's been taken ill and Mrs Kingsley's with him, but coffee would be an excellent idea. And if someone could bring a glass of water to the sitting room for my wife, I'd be most grateful.'

The man nodded, relieved to be given orders, and Mark followed Sophie into the sitting room, where she was searching in her handbag for a handkerchief.

'What a horrible thing to have happened!' she said unsteadily. 'Poor Daddy – he must be feeling terrible.'

'I'm sure the worst is over,' he said soothingly and, at the discreet tap on the open door, went to take the glass of water from a waiter. Sophie sipped at it slowly and gradually her breathing steadied.

But though he'd succeeded in comforting his wife, whose colour was now returning, Mark himself remained worried. Over the years he'd seen Peter Kingsley at countless parties, both as host and guest, and he'd always been in total control of himself. There must be some underlying problem that had contributed to his lack of it today.

After fifteen minutes, during which Sophie had become increasingly anxious to go to her parents, Charles and Lydia joined them in the sitting room. She jumped up to put an arm round her mother, who leant briefly against her.

'He's been vomiting,' Charles said tersely, 'but he's asleep now. He'll be fine when he wakes.'

'What's happening with the guests?' Lydia asked anxiously.

'I asked the staff to clear up the cake and serve coffee,' Mark replied. 'I think Mum's taken charge down there.'

'That's good of her, but I must go and have a word with them, explain it was the heat that upset him; he was under the midday sun for over an hour, with no head-covering.' She glanced at the others. 'Actually, I think it would look better if we all put in an appearance, if you wouldn't mind. Mark and Sophie needn't stay, but I must be there to say goodbye to our guests.'

'Of course we'll come.'

As they stepped out on to the terrace, Mark noticed that the sun had gone in and the air had taken on a metallic quality. Perhaps the break in the weather Lydia had feared was coming after all. Presenting a united front, the four of them walked back across the grass, pausing at the entrance to the marquee, where Lydia's hostess skills resurfaced.

'I'm so sorry, everyone. As you all know, Peter steadfastly refuses to wear a sunhat and I'm afraid the heat, followed by the rich food, proved too much for him. However, he's now much better and is resting in bed. He asked me to say how sorry he is for the upset, and hopes it won't have spoilt your enjoyment of the day.'

There was a polite murmur of assurance and understanding, and as the four of them started to circulate the atmosphere gradually lightened. By the time, half an hour later, that the guests began to disperse, it almost seemed as if the incident had been forgotten.

When the last of them had left, the Kingsleys and the Richmonds regathered in the sitting room.

'Well done, Lydia,' Charles said quietly. 'You were magnificent. You too, Margot, holding it all together in the immediate aftermath.'

Jonathan, after a significant glance from his wife, said hesitantly, 'I think perhaps we should be making a move too, if that's OK. We've arranged to meet some friends later.'

'Of course,' Lydia said quickly. 'And thank you so much for your support. And, of course, your present. They'll all be opened tomorrow and Peter will be in touch to thank you personally.' She turned to her daughter. 'Feel free to go too if you like, darling,' she added. 'I know it's been quite an ordeal for you, but it's over now.'

Sophie hesitated. 'Could I go up and see Daddy?'

'Better not. He's sleeping, anyway.'

'If we waited . . .?'

'Don't worry about him, Sophie,' Margot said firmly. 'Charles and I will stay with your mother for a while. You go home now and relax.'

'He'll phone you tomorrow,' Lydia repeated, and Sophie finally acquiesced.

The storm broke on their way home. In view of Sophie's upset, Mark had felt it wiser after all to do the driving himself, and it was as well that he did. The afternoon had grown progressively darker, more like late autumn than mid-August, and when they were about halfway a blinding zigzag of lightning flooded the car with silver light, followed instantly by an ear-numbing crack of thunder which seemed directly overhead. The car swerved momentarily under his hands.

'I hope Florence and Steph are back from the park,' Sophie said jerkily. 'She hates thunder.'

Then came the rain, glancing silver needles sluicing horizontally across the windscreen and drumming on the roof. Mark switched the wipers to full power but they fought a losing battle under the onslaught of water and he was driving almost blind.

Turning on his headlights, he moved cautiously into the slow lane as, he saw, drivers both behind him and ahead were doing. With a rare flash of fancy, he felt as though all the tensions of the day, unable to be contained any longer, had finally exploded.

Then, as suddenly as it had started, the rain ceased like a tap being turned off and the streaming windscreen was lit by an equally blinding ray of sunshine that reflected dazzlingly off the wet road. For once, Mark thought ironically, he really would be glad to get home.

In the months that followed, he was often to wonder if that afternoon had heralded the disintegration of the family.

THREE

Drumlee

A loud click penetrated Mark's sleep the next morning and he opened his eyes to see Nick bending over the fan heater. He straightened as Mark stirred.

'Sorry, did that wake you?'

'It's OK. What time is it?'

'Just gone seven thirty. Would you believe there's ice on the *inside* of the window?'

'I'd believe it!' Mark pulled a blanket up round his ears. 'God, what a country!'

'It's obvious they only come here in summer – no double glazing.' Nick glanced at his watch. 'I was wondering whether to take a shower now; do you think it would wake anyone?'

'I should risk it, and if it's still free, I'll go in straight after you. Might warm us up!'

Paula lay watching the daylight seep into the room. 'It looks like a lovely day,' she said sleepily.

'Excellent. I wonder if anyone will be up for a game of golf?'

'Seb might.' She paused. 'You were very restless in the night, darling. Didn't you sleep well?'

'I had trouble getting off, that's all.' Douglas's tone was dismissive.

But it wasn't all, Paula suspected. The tossing and turning had continued throughout the night, frequently waking her. He might deny it, but she knew something was on his mind and wished he'd share it with her. Perhaps once they were home again . . .

An appetizing smell of kippers met Mark and Nick as they came downstairs and they traced it to the large kitchen at the back of the house, where several members of the family were gathered. Sebastian, Danny and Natalie, seated at the scrubbed table, were halfway through their breakfast and Harry was on duty with the frying pan.

'Hi!' he greeted them cheerfully. 'Sleep well?'

'Like a log!' replied Nick, bending to kiss Natalie's cheek, and Mark let the answer stand for them both.

'There's a pair of kippers ready if anyone'd like them, but bacon and eggs are also on offer.'

'Kippers for me,' Mark said.

Nick added, 'Me too, please.'

'Kippers it is, then. Tea and coffee's on the side – help yourselves.'

The two men did so. 'Where's everyone else?' Mark enquired, taking his place at the table. 'Still in bed?'

'Jessica has a headache,' Harry said. 'I'm on breakfast duty, so I took her a tray when I did Mum and Dad's. When we're here we always give them breakfast in bed – their holiday treat.'

'And Helena?'

'Woke early, so she's gone for a walk,' Natalie replied. 'Said she'd be back around nine but she never has breakfast anyway, just a cup of coffee.' She glanced at Mark with a smile. 'Or perhaps you already know that!'

He smiled back non-committally as Harry came over with two plates of the golden fish. 'Scottish kippers – none better!' he announced with satisfaction.

Danny's egg-smeared plate showed he'd gone for the alternative and Sebastian, noting Mark's glance, said succinctly, 'Too many bones!'

Mark nodded. 'My – niece won't eat them either.' He'd almost said 'my daughter', and the thought of Florence brought the usual stab of pain. What would she be doing, this Saturday morning? Probably having breakfast in the kitchen at Dormers, fussed over by her grandmother. Oh God, Lydia! He hastily brought his thoughts back to the present.

Notwithstanding the bones, the kippers were delicious and Mark surprised himself by following them up with two slices of toast and marmalade. Normally, like Helena's, his breakfast consisted of a cup of coffee.

'So, what are the plans for today?' Sebastian asked, leaning back in his chair.

Harry shrugged. 'I doubt Jess will want to go far afield; she doesn't like the cold.'

'Well, you're welcome to join Danny and me. We're going for a bracing walk along the front, followed by a lunch of burger and chips.'

'Thanks; I'll join you for the walk, but I'll come back for lunch with Jess. How about you, Nat?'

'I'm going to introduce Nick to Drumlee, and I think Hellie's intending to show Adam around. We'll probably all end up at the Merlin for a bar lunch.'

'What about your parents?' Mark asked, concerned that their hosts might be left to their own devices.

'Oh, don't worry about them!' Harry said airily. 'We always separate during the day and meet up in the evenings. If I know Dad, he'll try to talk Mum into walking round the golf course with him.'

'I'll be happy to give him a game tomorrow,' Sebastian said.

They were still at the table half an hour later when Helena returned, looking decidedly more animated than when Mark had last seen her, skin glowing and hair tousled by the wind. She poured herself a mug of coffee and flopped down on the chair next to him.

'Ready for a tour of the metropolis?' she asked him.

'Raring to go.'

'It might surprise you,' Natalie cautioned. 'It's not your usual seaside town that shuts down out of season.'

To be honest, Mark wasn't sure how he'd imagined Drumlee; it had been dark when they'd arrived the previous evening and he'd been half asleep, but Sebastian's comment about the coast had indeed conjured up the picture of a string of houses offering bed and breakfast and shops selling buckets and spades, all boarded up for the winter. Wide of the mark, he now gathered, and this was confirmed half an hour later when he and Helena set out on their walk and he found himself in a street of solid stone houses, with the sea nowhere in sight. A plaque on the gatepost bore the name 'Touchstone'.

'What?' Helena challenged him, as he paused on the pavement.

'Somehow I'd imagined the sea to be just across the road,' he confessed with a smile.

'There are a couple of roads between, but we can smell it when the wind's in the right direction.'

'But it *is* a holiday town?'

'Oh yes, Drumlee has its fair share of visitors, but as Nat said, it's not dependent on them. Life goes on very comfortably all year round; there are clubs and a theatre and concert hall, as well as a thriving fishing industry. Part of the holiday we always looked forward to was going down to the harbour when the boats came in to watch them unload and weigh the fish, then buying some for supper. Those kippers you had would have been smoked locally.'

'So no buckets and spades and tatty souvenir shops? I'm quite disappointed!'

'Oh, buckets and spades are there if you want them, but the souvenirs are more likely to be tartan rugs or Rennie Mackintosh jewellery.' She paused. 'Still, there are more important things to discuss before we meet Nat and Nick for lunch.'

As they strolled down into the town, she answered such questions as had already occurred to him, including when and where they were supposed to have met, and volunteered more information about the family.

'Seb's been divorced for about two years,' she told him. 'Things had been difficult for a while, but it came to a head just before Harry and Jess's wedding, which was unfortunate to say the least. Danny lives with his mother and stepfather but spends most weekends with Seb.'

'Jessica seemed very quiet last night,' Mark ventured.

Helena frowned. 'To be honest, I'm not sure what to make of her. They live in Cheshire, so I don't see much of them. What I do know is that she's pretty talented – runs her own interior design business.'

They were approaching the town centre, and again Mark was pleasantly surprised. There was a spaciousness about it that gave an air of elegance to the wide streets, and ahead of them was a large square with flowerbeds in the centre.

As they drew near he saw these were filled with a sea of white blooms.

'Oh, how lovely!' Helena exclaimed. 'This must be part of Scotland's Snowdrop Festival. I've heard of it, but we've never been here for it.' She nodded towards a handsome building on the far side of the square. 'And that's the Merlin Hotel, where we'll be having lunch. In the meantime I want to buy something for the parents, so let's aim for the Mall.'

This proved to be an elegant indoor arcade and Mark, who loathed shopping, resigned himself to a boring half hour as he followed Helena in and out of a variety of shops.

'I want something red for their ruby wedding,' she said. 'Any ideas?'

'None,' he replied.

'What about your parents? Have they reached forty years?'

'No, two to go.' He paused, thinking wryly of himself and Sophie. 'I wonder how many of our generation will stick together that long?'

She gave a short laugh. 'Better not let the parents hear you say that, when you're my betrothed! But don't think it's always been a bed of roses for them; they separated for about a year when I was eleven.'

He looked at her in surprise. 'Really? Do you know why?'

She shook her head. 'It was never discussed, but Dad just upped and disappeared to his London office.'

'So – they don't live near London?'

'Something else I should have mentioned,' Helena chided herself. 'No, the family home's near Chester and Seb and Harry both work in the city.' She smiled. 'The boys stayed close to home and the girls fled the coop! Read what you will into that!'

'So Natalie's in London too?'

'Harrow, actually.' She broke off, staring into the shop window beside them. 'There!' she exclaimed in triumph. 'Exactly what I was looking for!'

In the centre of the window display was an elegant vase in ruby-red glass. Mark had another set of questions, but she'd already disappeared into the shop.

*   *   *

Jessica stood at her bedroom window watching Harry and his brother set off on their walk. God knew what they thought of her, all of them, especially the two new men who were joining the family. She hadn't exactly sparkled at dinner last night, and she'd noticed the fair one glance at her once or twice when Harry was trying to include her in the conversation. She could hardly have explained it was taking all her concentration simply to keep from vomiting.

Oh God, it was so *unfair*! she thought on a wave of helplessness. Why did this have to happen, now of all times? After months of hard work there were three really lucrative contracts coming to fruition, but it'd still take all her expertise to land them. She couldn't really afford even this week off, but it had been non-negotiable.

They'd not discussed starting a family since the early days. 'Don't forget you're marrying a career girl!' she'd told Harry when they first became engaged.

'And one I'm very proud of!' he'd replied. 'Don't worry, my love, I've no intention of tying you to the kitchen sink!'

And he had been as good as his word, always affording her work equal importance with his. But now both his sisters were engaged and if they started having babies, would it bring home to him that time was passing? She wanted a family, of course she did, but not yet, and not unplanned. Her career had from the start been built on meticulous planning, each move carefully evaluated in advance, and that had kept her head above water when many other businesses had sunk without trace.

But how could she possibly tell him she didn't want this baby whose arrival would be so inopportune? He'd be horrified, and, she thought miserably, rightly so. Nor could she expect any understanding from her mother, an Irish Catholic who herself had given birth to five children.

Oh God, she was going to be sick again! She turned from the window and hurried to the bathroom.

Drumlee promenade stretched for over a mile along the coast and was a popular venue with dog-walkers. There were seats at regular intervals but on this crisp morning only one was occupied, by a girl huddled in an anorak with the hood pulled up over her head. They nodded to her as they passed.

The tide was out, and on their left the sand lay ribbed and damp, sprinkled here and there with rock pools that glittered in the winter sun. Down here the wind was stronger, stinging tears into their eyes, and Harry wound his scarf more tightly round his neck. Danny was running ahead of them whooping joyously, arms outstretched in aeroplane mode.

'It's good to think I've a whole week of him to look forward to,' Sebastian commented.

Harry shot him a sideways glance. 'Was Diana quite amenable?'

'Grudging's a better description, but it's half-term so she'd no option. I think she was expecting we'd stay at home, though what difference that would make I don't know.'

Harry hesitated, carefully framing his next question. 'And how's that lady friend of yours?'

Seb's eyes were narrowed against the wind, their expression difficult to gauge. 'As well as the last time you asked.'

'Oh, come on! Any progress to report?'

'It's not a question of progress, Harry; the circumstances haven't changed.'

'They don't seem insurmountable to me. She's divorced, as are you, and from what you say the attraction's mutual. So what's the problem?'

Sebastian sighed heavily. 'Her children. I told you.'

'So you don't like her kids. Given time, they'd probably grow on you.'

'If I didn't strangle them first!'

'Boys or girls?'

'Girls, aged five and seven, so Danny's slap in the middle. They've only met once, but they immediately ganged up on him. Heaven help him if they were part of his family!'

'But it's not as though he lives with you,' Harry pointed out.

'But that's just the point,' Seb explained patiently. 'If Miriam and I got together, *they* would. He'd resent having to share me, especially as they'd be getting the lion's part.'

'Well, he shares his mother. He's got a little half-brother, hasn't he? Conceived, if I remember aright, while you and Diana were still nominally together.'

'That's different,' Sebastian argued, ignoring the last sentence. 'He'd been told Teddy was on the way, and to give Di her due she involved him in all the preparations for the baby, then let him help bath him and so on, so there was never a problem. Not like having two kids suddenly thrust on him, fully fledged as it were, and girls to boot!'

Harry kicked a pebble, watching it skitter across the promenade. 'Are you in love with her?' he asked.

Sebastian took his time replying. 'On the verge of, I think. Still time to pull back.'

'Have you slept together?'

He gave a bark of laughter. 'God, Harry, you don't beat about the bush, do you?'

'Well, have you?'

'Yes, but only very recently. A couple of times at most.'

'And it was good?'

'The best.'

Harry gave his brother a slap on the shoulder. 'Then go for it, bro, and the devil take the hindmost!' And before Seb could formulate a reply, he set off, whooping, after his nephew.

The Merlin Hotel, though imposing enough, was not as big as Mark had imagined when viewing it from across the square. The atmosphere on entering was at once both homely and contained, and he looked about him approvingly at the dark woodwork, pale walls and blue and cream patterned carpet.

His inspection was curtailed by a voice calling delightedly, 'Hellie!' and he turned to see an attractive woman in her fifties hurrying towards them and enveloping Helena in a hug. She then turned to him, her pleasant face wreathed in smiles.

'And this must be the lucky man! How do you do? I'm Lexie Mackay.'

'Adam Ryder,' he replied dutifully, taking the hand she held out. 'I've heard a lot about you.'

Lexie had turned back to Helena. 'It's been so long – you weren't here last summer, were you? Paula said something about sailing in the Aegean.'

With Jack, Helena remembered painfully. 'It couldn't hold a candle to Drumlee!' she said staunchly.

Lexie smiled, dismissing this with a wave of her hand. 'Well, it's only your parents who still come regularly, so all the more reason to celebrate when the whole family arrives. Will the boys be in for lunch?'

'No, they've taken Danny for a walk along the front. I think burgers and chips are the order of the day!'

Lexie laughed. 'Well, we'll see them at the celebration meal. Natalie and her young man are waiting for you in the bar.'

As indeed they were, surrounded by two or three couples who turned to greet Helena as they entered. Mark gathered from the flurry of introductions that they were locals who'd come to know the Crawfords over the years. Having arranged to meet them for a drink the following week, Natalie led the way to a window table, menu in hand, and they sat down to choose their meal.

'Did you see the snowdrops?' she asked, when they'd ordered and their drinks had arrived. 'Pretty spectacular, aren't they? In future I'm going to plant them en masse rather than dotted round the garden in clumps – make them more of a statement.'

'So you'll have a house with a garden?' Helena asked slyly, and laughed as Natalie flushed, glancing at Nick.

'Am I jumping the gun, when we're not even officially engaged?' she asked ruefully.

Nick patted her hand. 'Of course we'll have a garden!' he said.

Mark took a drink of his beer. 'When are you thinking of getting married?'

'Later this year, probably about September,' Natalie replied. 'What about you two? We'd better liaise, out of consideration to Dad's pocket! We'd be quite happy to foot the bill, but I know his pride will, insist he makes a substantial contribution.'

'We've not really discussed it,' Helena interposed. 'Everything's happened so quickly.'

'I believe you said you live in Chislehurst, Adam? Will you stay in that area, or move closer to London?'

'As Helena says, we haven't discussed it.' Remembering his ambivalence on leaving home, Mark wasn't even sure he still lived there himself, but such considerations were scheduled for his postponed walking holiday. For now, it would take him all his time to keep up the pretence he'd so unwillingly embarked on.

Fortunately the arrival of their meal ended the conversation, and as it progressed he watched Helena, seemingly relaxed as she chatted with her family. Was it his imagination that there was underlying tension, and if so did it stem from their charade? He'd come to know her slightly better during the morning, but still felt no empathy towards her.

They were on their coffee when a tall, dark man came in and made straight for their table.

'Well, well!' he exclaimed. 'My past revisited! Ma said you were here.'

'Blair!' Natalie jumped up, submitting to his hug with enthusiasm before moving aside for Helena, whose approach, Mark thought as he and Nick also rose, was more guarded. Natalie introduced them, they shook hands and he drew up a chair.

'So, tell me the news,' he invited. 'Wedding bells in the air all round, I gather, including Ruby ones! It was great to see your parents the other evening.'

'And how about you?' Helena asked lightly.

'Oh, I'm a confirmed bachelor. The two of you broke my heart!' Though he spoke jokingly, there was an undercurrent that caused Mark to look at him more closely.

'I hear Ailsa beat us all down the aisle,' Natalie said. 'Is she around?'

'She's at work but she'll be back later. She's running the local tourist board, so still roughly in the same business.'

'And married to the chef, no less!'

'Always a good move! Seriously, though, he's a great guy, Jean-Luc – a welcome addition to the family. We must—' He broke off as his mobile rang, and with a muttered apology answered it. 'Yes; yes, OK, I'll come now.'

He stood up regretfully. 'Sorry, this is what happens when I try to bunk off for a few minutes! We must arrange a proper get-together; I'll give you a call later.'

And with a smile that encompassed them all, he hurried from the room.

'So,' Nick teased, 'an old flame, was he?'

'Not really,' Natalie replied. 'It was very light-hearted – just a holiday romance. And we weren't alone; Ailsa says all the girls fall for Blair.'

'So I don't have to challenge him to pistols at dawn?'

Natalie smiled, patting his hand. 'Definitely not worth getting up for!'

Half a mile away, the girl in a hooded anorak turned into one of the B&Bs along the front and went up to her room. Closing the door behind her, she sat down on the bed, drew a deep breath and took out her mobile.

FOUR

Kent

The storm was long past by the time Charles and Margot Richmond set out for home, though the roads were still treacherous, with large puddles lurking in potholes that splashed tides of water over the unwary. It was a short drive, since the two families lived only a few miles apart, and most of it had passed in a reflective silence. It wasn't until they were approaching their own village that Margot said, 'Well, what did you make of that?'

Charles, who had been busy with his own thoughts, merely grunted in reply.

'Obviously he was drunk,' Margot continued, following her own line of thought, 'but something a good deal more serious lay behind it, you mark my words.'

Though he too had been shaken by Peter's behaviour, Charles tried to downplay it. 'You're reading too much into it,' he maintained. 'He'd been drinking on an empty stomach in the hot sun and without a hat – asking for trouble.'

'How long have we known Peter Kingsley?' Margot demanded rhetorically. 'Have we *ever* seen him the worse for drink?'

'It's never been his sixtieth before.' Charles turned into their driveway to a snort of derision from his wife. She got out of the car and by the time he joined her had unlocked the front door and was stepping out of her shoes with a sigh of relief.

'I'll have a word with Lydia tomorrow,' she continued, 'and suggest she gets him to see a doctor.'

'Oh, come on, Margot, don't go putting the wind up her! After a good night's sleep he'll be right as rain. The poor bloke's entitled to one lapse in a previously blameless existence.'

'And what do you make of the storm of tears, once you'd got him upstairs?'

He should have known better than to tell her that, Charles reflected. 'Remorse,' he replied. 'Shame at having made a spectacle of himself in front of his guests.'

She shook her head decidedly, patting her hair in front of the mirror before turning into the sitting room. 'That might have played a part, but there's something underlying all this, and the sooner it's out in the open, the better it will be.'

'For whom?' Charles scoffed. 'You, to satisfy your curiosity?'

'For Peter, of course. Not to mention Lydia, and poor little Sophie. She was distraught.'

'Well, I don't know about you, but *I'm* in need of a drink, and a strong one at that. Unlike old Pete, champagne does nothing either to or for me; might as well have been drinking water. Can I get you something?'

She was standing in front of the fireplace, staring down at the large vase of roses that screened the empty grate. 'Yes, I could do with a fresh, clean taste myself. Pour me a G and T, would you?'

He nodded and went to the kitchen for ice and lemon, his mind still on his friend. Was she right? he wondered uneasily. Was it more than the drink that had caused Peter's disintegration? Not a question he wanted to probe.

'I'll certainly phone in the morning,' Margot reiterated as he returned to the sitting room. 'But I'll wait to see what she says before mentioning the doctor.'

Charles breathed a sigh of relief. 'Good thinking,' he said.

Sunday morning, and as always during their lie-ins, Florence arrived clutching her teddy bear and climbed on to their bed.

'The clock's pointing to getting-up time,' she announced triumphantly.

Mark groaned and pulled the pillow over his head, part of the weekly routine, and with a giggle she pulled it off again. Beside him Sophie sat up, running her fingers through her hair.

'How soon do you think I can ring Mum?' she asked distractedly.

'She said they'd phone you,' Mark reminded her. 'Just relax, darling, and I'll bring you a cup of tea.'

'How can I relax, until I know how Daddy is?'

'He'll be fine. Stop worrying.'

She gave an exclamation of annoyance and swung her feet to the ground. 'I'm going for a shower,' she said.

Mark sighed, battling irritation. He supposed it was natural for her to worry, but the previous evening had been spent going over and over the incident and discussing possible causes for Peter's uncharacteristic behaviour. He'd no intention of letting it dominate the day ahead as well. Resignedly he too got out of bed and lifted Florence to the floor.

'Come on, poppet,' he said, 'let's go and see what we can find for breakfast.'

When her daughter phoned just after nine thirty, Lydia was determinedly upbeat. 'Oh, he's fine, darling. Nursing a sore head – no more than he deserves! – but otherwise fine.'

'Can I speak to him?' Sophie asked.

'He's in the shower at the moment,' Lydia lied, in response to her husband's quick shake of the head, 'and as you can imagine, feeling a little embarrassed about what happened. Give him a day or two to regain his equilibrium, then I know he'd love to hear from you.'

However, when Margot rang an hour later Peter had retired to the garden with the Sunday papers and she was able to speak more freely.

'I *am* concerned about him, Margot, no use denying it. I think, between the two of us, that this might have been coming on for some time.'

'That's what I suspected,' Margot replied, with unworthy satisfaction. 'Are you free to talk?'

'Not really; he's in the garden, but he might wander in any time. Could we meet for coffee next week?'

'An excellent idea. I have to go into Sevenoaks on Tuesday; how about meeting at Malabar about eleven?'

'That would be perfect. Thanks, Margot. See you then.'

As she replaced the receiver, Lydia wondered just how frank she could be with her friend. Some of her worries wouldn't be easy to talk about, but Margot was like the sister she'd never had, and Lydia felt sure she could count on her discretion. Feeling slightly better, she turned her thoughts to the Sunday lunch.

Charles had also been worrying about Peter, though for much more complicated reasons. He sometimes felt he was in a love–hate relationship with this man who'd been a close friend for over forty years.

They'd met at university and from the first Charles's liking for Peter was tinged with envy: he was brighter and better looking than himself, more popular with their fellow students and – perhaps chief cause of his resentment – came from a much more affluent background, evidenced by his clothes, his easy manner and the gleaming sports car in which he'd arrived at university. But for some reason Charles never understood, it was he whom Peter chose as his closest friend.

Before long, that friendship was put severely to the test, though Peter remained unaware of it, as he did of much else as the years went by. It began at a party given by a fellow student which, due to a previous engagement, Peter had been unable to attend. The host's sister had brought a friend with her, a startlingly pretty girl called Lydia Crowther, and Charles had experienced a *coup de foudre* from which, though no one suspected it, he'd never fully recovered.

Overcoming his normal reserve, he'd approached her on some pretext and, as their conversation continued, became more and more enthralled by her. They'd spent the rest of the evening together, and, since she lived locally, she agreed to go to a pop concert with him the following week. He'd been suffused with a wild, ecstatic happiness, hardly daring to believe his luck and suddenly convinced that all that had been lacking in his life was now within his grasp.

It was as they were leaving the party that, by some malevolent chance, they met Peter in the university quad and, since there was no help for it, Charles introduced them, aware even as he did so of the instant attraction that sparked between them.

Seeking to establish his prior claim, he mentioned that they were going to the concert the next week.

'Oh, I heard it was on,' Peter exclaimed. 'It should be great
– I envy you.'

And to Charles's horror, Lydia said lightly, 'Then why not
come with us?' Belatedly she'd turned to Charles with that
heart-stopping smile of hers. 'That would be OK, wouldn't
it?'

Six weeks later they were engaged, news which Peter
imparted privately to Charles before the announcement.
'Hope I haven't stepped on your toes, old boy,' he said
apologetically. 'I know it was you who introduced us – for
which I'll be eternally grateful – but you'd only met that
evening, hadn't you? Lydia assured me there was nothing
between you.'

'Nothing at all,' Charles had muttered from the depths of
a broken heart, a condition he'd continued to nurse in secret
until, about a year later, he'd met Margot – dear, dependable
Margot, whose brisk, no-nonsense affection had held him
together on many occasions throughout their marriage.

Though he'd now arrived at the golf club, Charles continued
to sit in the car, hands still on the steering wheel as he thought
back over their long friendship. A belated wave of shame came
over him and he bitterly regretted all those snide comments
that Peter had good-naturedly taken as jokes, culminating in
his own recent totally unforgivable behaviour. Remembering
the sobs that had convulsed his friend on Saturday, he was
overcome with a sick dread that he might be responsible – a
poor way, he thought wretchedly, to repay all Peter's generosity
over the years.

He drew back his shoulders and took a deep breath. No,
that couldn't be the cause of his distress; he'd been ill – a
combination of over-indulgence and sunstroke, no doubt – and
he'd soon be his old, easy-going self again. Nonetheless, to
ease that niggling worm of doubt, from now on Charles determined to support him in any way he could. Which, all things
considered, Peter might well be in need of.

A tap on the window made him start, and he turned to see
his golf partner smiling at him through the glass.

'Going to sit there all day,' he enquired jovially, 'or are we
going to have that game?'

Thankfully Charles put aside his worries and got out of the car.

It was a blisteringly hot afternoon. Sophie lay back with closed eyes, soaking up the sunshine and barely registering the shrieks of excitement as the two little girls jumped in and out of the paddling pool.

Stella Jordan emerged through the patio doors and handed her a glass of iced lemonade before sinking on to the lounger beside her. 'Now this,' she proclaimed, stretching out her long, tanned legs, 'is how to spend a Monday afternoon!'

Sophie nodded absently. She was still worried about her father, but though she frequently complained about her husband's shortcomings, she was less inclined to discuss his.

'Oh, I meant to tell you,' Stella was continuing. 'I'll have to let you down about Bournemouth, I'm afraid; Rex has decided he wants to come with us. Sorry about that.'

Sophie's disappointment was tinged with annoyance, since this meant handing Mark the victory on a plate. 'He doesn't usually play the family man,' she remarked ungraciously.

Stella gave a brief laugh. 'How right you are! But he's been having a pretty hectic time at work and thinks the sea air will restore him. I doubt if we'll see much of him – he'll be off playing golf most of the time.'

Sophie and Stella had met on a cordon bleu course that both sets of parents had insisted their daughters attend on leaving school, though apart from turning them into excellent cooks it had had no bearing on their future careers – or lack of them.

They lost contact soon afterwards, and in the years that followed Sophie drifted into marriage with Mark and Stella met and married Rex Jordan who, though until then a confirmed bachelor, had fallen for her quick wit and considerable charm. Fifteen years her senior, he was a wealthy and successful businessman who believed that as long as his wife had unlimited access to his credit cards he was discharging his duties towards her.

The two of them met again by chance pram-pushing in a local park, and, having discovered their daughters had been

born within months of each other, repaired to a nearby coffee
shop for an update on the intervening years.

'I'm a trophy wife, and that suits me fine!' Stella had laughingly claimed, admitting that, though fond of him, it was her
husband's lifestyle she was in love with, and she enjoyed
playing the part of the glamorous hostess.

Since that fortuitous meeting three years ago they'd become
firm friends and met on a regular basis, often with their daughters, though never their husbands, in tow.

'You don't mind, do you?' Stella prompted after a minute.
'About Bournemouth, I mean? We can go another time.'

'I *was* looking forward to it,' Sophie admitted.

'Then let's make a definite date. How about October
half-term? It might not be beach weather, but there'll be
plenty to do.'

Sophie brightened. 'OK, that would be good.'

Stella paused, moving a cube of ice round her glass with
one finger. 'In the meantime, I'll tell you a secret that I was
saving for Bournemouth.'

'Sounds intriguing.'

'It is, rather. I've got an admirer!' She sat back to watch
her friend's reaction.

Removing her sunglasses, Sophie turned to look at her.
'You've what?'

'You heard – got an admirer! I met him a couple of weeks
ago – and Sophie, he's gorgeous!'

'But how – I mean what . . .?'

Stella gave an excited laugh 'I know! I can hardly believe
it myself!'

Sophie sat up, swinging her legs to the grass and turning
to face her friend. 'I think you'd better start at the beginning,'
she said.

'His name's Lance Grenville. Lance! How about that? Like
something out of *Pulp Fiction*, isn't it?'

'Or King Arthur,' Sophie rejoined.

'Well, we were at some stuffy cocktail do of Rex's, and he
was off in a corner networking as usual. I noticed this man
watching me from across the room and after a while he came
over and we got talking. It turned out he's an investment

banker, divorced, no children – though I learned that later.
And in the course of conversation the new James Bond film
came up. I said I hadn't seen it and he said nor had he, why
not go together?'

Stella paused, glancing at her friend and trying to gauge
her reaction. 'It was so unexpected, Sophie, coming out of the
blue like that – I was completely dumbstruck. Eventually I
made some facetious remark about my husband not approving,
and he said, "Then don't tell him!" Simple as that!'

She laughed again. 'I don't know about you, but I've never
been picked up before, and I really didn't know what to say.'

'But you said yes?' Sophie guessed, and Stella nodded.

'Honestly, I felt like a scarlet woman! I told Rex it was a
girls' night out and I might be late back as we were eating
after the film – which Lance had already suggested – and I
felt really guilty when he swallowed it without question. But
let's face it, Rex, bless him, has never lit any fires in me.'

'Whereas Lance does?'

'Potentially. It's very early days.'

'So how far has this – affair, if that's what it is, progressed?'

'Hardly at all as yet. We duly saw the film – which was very
good, by the way – then went on to a chichi restaurant – very
small, only ten tables, presumably so we'd see no one we knew.
But over the meal the conversation was a bit stilted, and to be
honest I didn't really enjoy it. I was on edge, expecting him to
suggest any minute that we went to bed together.'

'And he didn't?'

She shook her head.

'Would you have done, if he had?'

Stella flushed, tipped back her glass and finished the last
warm drops of her lemonade. 'To be honest I don't know; I
wasn't sure whether to be relieved or disappointed when he
didn't even kiss me goodnight. In fact, I thought the whole
thing had just fizzled out.'

Sophie swung her legs back on to the lounger and lay down
again, replacing her sunglasses. 'Have you heard from him
since?' she asked after a minute.

'We had lunch last week while Rosie was at Summer
School.'

'And?'

'And nothing, really. When he left, he just said he'd be in touch. But I can't stop thinking about him.' She paused, and when Sophie didn't speak, added, 'Do you think I'm making too much of it?'

'I honestly don't know, Stella; you're in a much better position to judge than I am. But to be brutally honest, if he *has* "got designs on you", there's obviously only one thing he's after, and you have to decide if it's worth taking the risk. You've a great deal to lose if Rex gets wind of it.'

Stella gazed into her empty glass. 'Suppose the positions were reversed, and this had happened to you. What would you do?'

Sophie lifted her shoulders and let them fall. 'I'd probably risk it,' she said, surprising herself. 'As I've told you often enough, life with Mark is pretty boring – except in bed, to give him his due.' She smiled suddenly. 'But I reckon a little bit of spice on the side would go down a treat!'

By eleven o'clock on Tuesday morning, Lydia had changed her mind several times about meeting Margot. She'd probably let her imagination run riot; yesterday Peter had gone to work seemingly restored to his normal self, though still pale and with pouches under his eyes. However, he'd been determinedly cheerful and she didn't want to dent his wellbeing by insisting he saw the doctor, even if that would have relieved her mind.

She was still dithering when she parked the car. Margot had been coming to town anyway, she argued to herself; it wasn't as if she'd come in specially. If she phoned and said something had come up, it wouldn't be a big deal. But it would to her, Lydia admitted helplessly; she'd be denying herself the chance of Margot's wise counsel, on which she'd come to rely over the years.

Peter, bless him, had been aware of her own lack of gravitas from the first. 'My little scatterbrain', he'd called her. Margot, on the other hand, though only a year or two older, was of a different calibre, more serious-minded, more – sensible. Their friendship was on a different level from that of the crowd of women with whom Lydia had coffee, played bridge and went to the gym. Though fond of them and enjoying their company, she could never confide in any of them. And if ever she'd needed some good advice, it was now.

Still a little reluctantly, Lydia set off for their appointment.

Margot too had been anticipating their meeting with less than her usual enthusiasm, being unwilling to admit the extent of her own worry to Lydia whom, she reflected with wry humour, she seemed to have been protecting for the last forty years.

She and Charles had married two years after the Kingsleys, and since their husbands were close friends the two women, though total opposites, had to some extent been thrown together. Margot's initial irritation at what she'd considered Lydia's 'flibbertigibbetry' soon softened to fondness, with an additional sense of guilt when her friend continued to suffer miscarriages while she produced two healthy sons.

She'd been almost as delighted as her parents when Sophie finally put in an appearance, and understood, though she couldn't condone, the leniency with which she'd been brought up, always getting her own way and being given everything she asked for. The result, of course, was a thoroughly spoilt and selfish young woman, and on the rare occasions when she couldn't sleep, Margot worried about how her son was coping. The two of them, though friends all their lives, had never seemed to have that extra spark so vital for a happy marriage. But that was a worry for another day.

'I've ordered you an espresso and a buttered teacake,' was Lydia's greeting to Margot as she joined her.

Margot smiled. 'How well you know me! Thanks.' She laid her purchases on an adjacent chair. 'So, how's Peter, now he's had a few days to recover?'

Lydia sighed, toying with the cutlery on the table. 'He says he's OK and he went back to work yesterday. He spent Sunday phoning all the guests, thanking them for their presents and apologizing for the hiatus.'

'Yes, we had a call.'

'You and Charles were marvellous on Saturday,' Lydia said fervently. 'I don't know what we'd have done without you.'

'We were glad to help, but you carried it off beautifully, returning to the marquee and speaking to everyone.' She paused. 'You're still worried about him, though?'

'Sometimes I am, then I tell myself I'm imagining things.' She broke off as the waitress materialized, unloading their coffee and cakes from her tray.

'You said it had been coming on for some time,' Margot reminded Lydia as the waitress moved away.

'Yes, but nothing I could really put a finger on. He just seemed – different at times.'

'Different in what way?'

'Not as demonstrative as he used to be.'

Margot said carefully, 'By "demonstrative", do you mean affectionate?'

Lydia bit her lip. 'I suppose so, yes.' She gave a forced little laugh. 'But after all, he *is* sixty.'

Margot raised her eyebrows. 'And what exactly has that got to do with it?'

Lydia flushed. 'Well, you know what I mean. At our age, we don't make mad passionate love every night, do we?'

'Not every night, certainly.'

Lydia looked up quickly. 'You mean you—?' She broke off, her flush deepening.

'Lydia darling, are you asking if Charles and I still make love? Because if so, the answer is of course we do, though not, as you pointed out, every night.' She smiled. 'Or anything like it.' She studied her friend's downcast face. 'Are you saying you and Peter don't?' she asked gently.

'We cuddle, of course,' Lydia said with difficulty. 'And he's always perfectly sweet to me. But it's a long time since . . .' Her voice tailed off.

'Oh, my love, I'm so sorry. Have you talked about it?'

She shook her head. 'I tried once, but it upset him, I could see. He said, almost desperately, "You do know, don't you, how very much I love you?" As though I'd accused him of not doing, which wasn't what I meant at all.' She paused and added in a low voice, 'I'm wondering if he's found someone else.'

'Oh, Lyddie, I'm sure not!' Margot said emphatically. 'He adores you, anyone can see that. Possibly it's a medical problem and he's too embarrassed to go to the doctor. You know what men are like.'

Lydia nodded, but without conviction.

'Would you like Charles to have a word with him?'

'No!' she said sharply. Then, 'Well, not about that, though of course if it happened to come up . . .'

'Consider it done,' Margot said firmly.

FIVE

Drumlee

I t was at Sunday breakfast that Mark made his first faux pas. He had only been half-listening as the conversation turned to a new and highly recommended restaurant that had opened in Mayfair.

'It costs the earth,' Helena was saying, 'but apparently it's worth it.'

'Get Adam to take you on your birthday,' Natalie suggested. Then, when he didn't respond, she prompted, 'Adam?'

He looked up quickly. 'Sorry; yes?'

'How about taking Hellie to The Crimson Plumes as a birthday treat?'

'Sure,' he said, 'good idea; when is it?'

There was a brief, surprised silence, then Natalie gave a short laugh. 'You don't know?'

'Don't look so horrified, Nat,' Helena broke in quickly. 'We've only known each other six weeks, remember; we've not covered all the bases yet.' Then, to Mark, 'It's the third of March, darling. Time to start saving up!'

The moment had passed, but the conversation lodged in Natalie's mind. A couple of hours later, as she and Nick battled their way along the cliff path in the teeth of a bitingly cold wind, she said suddenly, 'What did you make of Adam not knowing Hellie's birthday?'

'Well, as she said, they've not known each other long.'

'Exactly, and that's another thing; we'd never even heard of him until a few weeks ago, and he doesn't strike me as the impulsive type.'

'Love can overwhelm the most prosaic of us!' Nick proclaimed facetiously.

'But they don't *behave* like an engaged couple. I sometimes wonder if they're really engaged at all.'

'Oh, come on, darling!' Nick protested. 'Just because they're not all over each other like we are doesn't mean—'

'We're *not* all over each other!' Natalie interrupted indignantly.

He laughed. 'My point precisely. So perhaps *we* don't behave like an engaged couple either.'

She didn't pursue it, but as they reserved their breath for the battle against the wind she continued to think about her sister, her mind going back over the years to when they were children. They'd never been close, Helena resenting her for usurping her own place as baby of the family, the only girl with two elder brothers. Many was the time she'd been pinched, tripped up as she ran in the garden and jeered at when she cried. And years later, Helena had purloined more than one of her boyfriends, even gatecrashing an early flirtation with Blair Mackay. Come to that, Natalie thought suddenly, she wouldn't put it past her to flaunt a fake engagement, simply to steal her thunder.

'I don't know about you,' Nick said, breaking into her thoughts, 'but I've had enough of this. How about turning back and stopping at the first pub we come to for lunch?'

'Good idea,' she said thankfully.

They started back along the path, the buffeting wind now aiding rather than impeding their progress, and had almost reached the end of it when they heard running footsteps behind them and a breathless voice called, 'Excuse me – I think you dropped this!'

They turned to see a girl in a hooded anorak approaching, holding a pink woollen scarf.

'No,' Natalie said, 'it's not mine.'

'Oh – sorry!'

The newcomer was pale and shivering with cold, and the medic in Natalie came to the forc. 'Are you all right?' she asked, taking in the thin jeans and trainers. 'You're not exactly equipped for this weather.'

A rueful smile. 'No, I didn't realize it would be quite so cold.'

'You don't live here?'

She shook her head.

'Then you should go back to your hotel,' Natalie decreed, 'and spend the rest of the day in front of the fire. Doctor's orders!'

'You're a doctor?'

'A GP, yes.' She glanced at Nick, standing silently by her side. 'So is my fiancé.'

'Well, it's good advice, but I'm staying at a B and B and not allowed back till five.'

'But that's ridiculous in this weather!' Natalie exclaimed, glancing about her. There was no one else in sight. 'Are you here by yourself?'

The girl nodded, her eyes filling with tears.

Natalie reached a unilateral decision, and with a quick apologetic glance at Nick said firmly, 'Well, we're just going for a pub lunch. You'd better come with us.'

She felt his movement of protest as their companion gave a little gasp. 'Oh no, I don't want to . . .'

'Nonsense. You need some hot food inside you, and so do we. I'm Natalie, by the way, and this is Nick.'

'Ellie,' the girl said in a whisper.

'Then come along, Ellie, and over lunch you can tell us why you chose to come alone to Scotland in the depths of winter.'

The Thistle was a small, cosy pub, and out of season its lunchtime clientele consisted mainly of those who worked in nearby shops and offices. Nick secured them a table near the fire and went to the bar for a menu. Local laws varied about the legal age for alcohol; Natalie hoped this pub didn't insist on drinkers being twenty-one. She doubted Ellie was that old, or, come to that, even eighteen, but she'd asked for a shandy, which was pretty innocuous.

Nick returned with the drinks and a couple of menus. 'I'm going native!' Natalie announced after glancing through it. 'Cullen skink and a crusty roll will go down a treat. It's a soup,' she added for Ellie's benefit, 'and a very good one, made with smoked haddock, potatoes, onions and cream.'

'Sounds delicious,' Ellie murmured, holding out her hands

to the fire. Its nearness had brought colour back to her cheeks and she'd shaken her hair free of the hood. It hung almost to her shoulders, sleek and brown, and Natalie saw with faint surprise that she was pretty.

'Will you join me then,' she prompted, 'or would you rather have something else? One of the famous Scotch pies, for instance?'

'That's what I'm going for,' Nick informed them.

'I'd like the soup, please,' Ellie said, 'but I'll pay for it.' She reached for her bag.

'Nonsense,' Natalie said firmly. 'We invited you to join us, so you're our guest.'

'But really, I—'

'Non-negotiable,' Nick said, and went back to the bar to order their meal.

'So,' Natalie began, leaning back in her chair and sipping her wine, 'what made you decide to come to the frozen north in February?'

Ellie's eyes brimmed again and she bit her lip. Natalie waited, neither pressing nor exempting her from answering, and after a minute she said, 'It was a favourite place of Mum's; she was always talking about it.' A pause as her hands clenched together tightly in her lap. 'She died just before Christmas,' she added, barely audibly.

Impulsively Natalie reached across, closing her own hand over the clenched ones. 'Oh, I'm so sorry.'

Ellie gave her head a little shake and straightened her shoulders. 'I know it would have been more sensible to wait till spring, but I . . . needed to get away.'

'What about your father? Is he still alive?'

A tremor went through her. 'I've never met him,' she said. 'He . . . left before I was born.'

Difficult ground, Natalie warned herself. 'But you must have someone?' she asked tentatively.

'My gran,' Ellie answered, to her profound relief. 'We've always lived with her, Mum and me, and Gramps too, of course, till he died two years ago.' She paused, then went on, 'My boyfriend wants me to move in with him, but I know Gran wouldn't like it, and anyway now's not the time.'

'No,' Natalie agreed, seeing with relief that Nick was making his way back. She'd probed enough into what was none of her concern.

For the rest of the meal conversation was intentionally light, but Natalie, having instigated the relationship, felt obscurely responsible for the girl; it would be difficult, after this lunch, to abandon her to her lonely grief.

Ellie herself was growing increasingly relaxed as the meal progressed. 'You've not said why *you're* here at this time of year,' she remarked as she finished the last of her soup.

Natalie smiled. 'Too true, we haven't. Well, my parents met here years ago and we've always come back for holidays, though in the summer, of course. But it'll be their fortieth wedding anniversary on Tuesday, so the family has gathered for that.'

Ellie's hand stilled momentarily over her soup bowl. Then she asked brightly, 'Are there a lot of you, then?'

'Two brothers and a sister, with various appendages.'

'Of which I'm one!' Nick said.

Ellie smiled. 'It must be great to have a large family. I saw two men with a little boy yesterday, on the prom. There aren't many visitors around – would they be your relations?'

'Doubtless my brothers Sebastian and Harry, with Danny, who belongs to Seb.' Natalie looked at her watch. 'Which reminds me, we're supposed to be meeting them for indoor bowls at two thirty. We'd better make a move.'

Ellie immediately shrugged on her anorak and retrieved her bag. 'Are you sure I can't pay for my lunch? I'd feel much happier.'

'Not a chance.'

'Then thanks once again, it's very kind of you.'

As they walked towards the door Natalie asked suddenly, 'Have you got a mobile?' and was aware of Nick's questioning look.

'Yes.'

'Give me your number, and perhaps we can do this again.'

Ellie's face lit up. 'That would be great – but I'll certainly be paying next time!' She glanced down at the pink scarf she was holding. 'What do you think I should do about this?' she asked uncertainly. 'Hand it in somewhere?'

'Well, it doesn't look very expensive,' Natalie replied, tying her own scarf. 'I doubt if anyone will bother to report it, but to salve your conscience you could phone the police and say you found it. Ten to one they'll just tell you to keep it unless you hear to the contrary.'

Ellie nodded. 'Right, I'll do that,' she said.

They parted on the windy street, but as Ellie watched them walk away she was well aware she wouldn't be contacting the police or anyone else. The scarf was, in fact, her own.

Sebastian said abruptly, 'Have you noticed anything about the old man?'

They were walking back from bowls in the cold darkness and Harry, who'd been about to catch up with the others, fell back again. 'No. What?'

'I don't know – he just doesn't seem himself. What's more, I get the impression Mum's worried about him.'

'Well, I must say I've not picked up on that. Been too busy trying to fathom Jess out,' he added ruefully.

'At least she came to the bowls.'

'Only because I more or less dragged her. But to get back to the old man, what makes you think something's wrong?'

'For one thing he's hardly eating anything, and you know what an appetite he has normally. Once I registered that, I studied him more closely and several times, instead of joining in the general conversation, he seemed to retreat into a world of his own – and not a pleasant one, by the look of him.'

'Now you've got *me* worried! Do you think he's ill, then?'

'Either that, or there's something on his mind.'

'And he's keeping it quiet till after the anniversary?'

'God, I hadn't got that far, but you could be right.'

'Do you reckon we should have a word with him, in case it's something we could deal with? On the work front, for instance?'

Sebastian shook his head, closing the gate behind them. 'Just keep a watching brief and we can discuss it again later.'

He and Harry joined the others in the hall, where they were stepping out of boots and hanging their coats on the stand.

'Where's Danny?' he asked, looking round.

'He went shooting off upstairs the minute he got in,' Helena reported. 'Probably needed the loo.'

'No, he went just before we left the sports centre. I'd better make sure he's OK.'

Sebastian started up the stairs, and on reaching the second floor was surprised to find the door of the room he shared with his son firmly closed. He was even more surprised to hear Danny's voice coming from behind it.

Frowning, he threw the door open. Danny turned swiftly, his face flushing bright red and a mobile phone Seb had never seen before clamped to his ear.

'Who are you speaking to?' he demanded, striding towards the boy and seizing the phone.

Danny's mouth trembled. 'Mummy,' he whispered.

Sebastian stared at him as panicky thoughts of sexual grooming faded. 'Off you go downstairs,' he said more quietly, and waited till the child had scuttled out of the room before lifting the phone to his own ear.

'Diana?'

'Still the forceful father, I see.'

'How long has he had this phone?'

'Since last week.'

'I thought we decided he should wait till he's at least seven.'

'Circumstances change,' she said.

'And exactly what does that mean?'

'I didn't know you proposed to take him hundreds of miles away.'

'For God's sake, Di! You make it sound as though I've kidnapped him! And I suppose you told him not to mention it to me?'

'Actually, yes.'

'Teaching him to be deceitful. Wonderful!'

'Oh, come off your high horse, Sebastian! I simply arranged to call him at five o'clock each evening, to check he was all right.'

'And why shouldn't he be?'

'He might have been missing me.'

'Did he say he had?'

A brief pause. 'No.'

'Then there's no need to disrupt his holiday any further, is there? He'll be home this time next week, dammit! In the meantime, I'm not having him panic every day in case he can't get back in time for your call.' He paused, but she didn't speak. 'All right?'

'I suppose so,' she said sulkily.

'Good. I'll bring him home on Sunday, as arranged. And should a cyclone hit Drumlee before then, you'll be the first to know.'

He ended the call and, going to the dressing table, leaned on the glass, staring at his angry face in the mirror. How was it that his ex-wife still had the ability to push his buttons?

Despising himself, he flipped the phone open again. There'd been two previous calls, on Friday and Saturday, both at five p.m. and both from Diana. Enough. He switched it off, put it in the chest of drawers and went downstairs.

Apart from the first night, Danny had his meal before the rest of the family, and as usual Sebastian sat with him while he ate it.

'I'm not cross with you, kiddo,' he told him, ruffling the boy's hair. 'It was just that I didn't know you had a phone or who you were speaking to. But it's all right; Mummy explained and she's not going to bother calling again, though if you want to speak to her at any time, just let me know, OK?'

'OK,' Danny repeated, and, relief flooding his face, he attacked his meal with gusto.

It being Sunday, dinner that evening was roast pork, which necessitated Douglas carving at the table, and Harry, alerted by his brother, noticed to his dismay that his father's hands shook slightly. How could he have missed this? he castigated himself.

His attention switched as Jessica suddenly pushed back her chair. 'I'm awfully sorry; I'm not at all hungry,' she said in a rush. 'If you don't mind, I'll wait for you in the other room.'

Paula looked up anxiously. 'Don't you feel well, dear? Would you like me—?'

'I'm fine,' Jess interrupted, smiling determinedly all round.

'It's my own fault – the ice I had at bowls spoiled my appetite. Please, just enjoy your meal.' And she hurried from the room.

Harry, staring furiously down at his plate and concentrating on keeping his temper, failed to notice the exchanged looks between the female members of his family.

Feeling tensions ought to be lowered, Natalie spoke into the short silence. 'Nick and I had an interesting experience at lunchtime,' she volunteered, and saw thankfully that she'd everyone's attention.

'Well, don't keep us in suspense!' Helena prompted.

'A girl came up to us on the cliff path with a scarf she thought I'd dropped, but it wasn't mine. She wasn't dressed warmly enough and was literally shivering with cold.'

'So Doctor Nat took her under her wing,' Nick put in.

Sebastian laughed. 'Nat and her lame ducks!' he said fondly.

Natalie ignored them both. 'I suggested she went home and warmed up by the fire, but she's staying at a B and B and had to be out of the house till five. Imagine, in this weather! So I invited her to join us for lunch. It was a sad story: her mother, who was a single parent, died at Christmas. She'd apparently loved Drumlee and often spoke of it, and the girl – Ellie – felt that being here might somehow bring her closer.'

'You mean she's here by herself?' Mark asked.

'Yes; I was relieved to hear she lives with her grandmother and has a boyfriend, so she's not entirely alone, but I felt really sorry for her. She was so interested to hear about you all, not having much family of her own.' She glanced at her brothers. 'She thinks she saw you with Danny on the prom yesterday.'

Seb looked puzzled, but Harry, determinedly joining in the conversation, nodded. 'There was a girl on one of the benches. I noticed her because no one else was about.'

'What does she do for an evening meal?' Paula wondered.

'Probably goes to a pub or café,' Nick replied. 'I didn't get the impression she's hard up; after all, she could afford the fare to come here and stay a few days, and she tried to pay for her lunch. Her clothes mightn't have been appropriate for the weather but they were of reasonable quality.'

'Nonetheless, it must be pretty grim, alone up here after a

bereavement,' Natalie said. 'I took her mobile number and suggested we meet later in the week.'

'If she was interested in the family, perhaps we could all meet her?' Paula suggested. 'Invite her here for lunch one day, so she doesn't feel so alone?'

'That would be great, Mum,' Natalie exclaimed. 'Let's fix a day now and I can give her a ring, prove it wasn't an empty promise.'

'Oh, and by the way, folks,' Seb put in, 'on the subject of meals, we won't be wanting dinner tomorrow; we're meeting up with Blair, Ailsa and her husband. Monday's their quietest day, so that suits them best.'

'Very well. How about Wednesday for Ellie, then?' Paula suggested. 'Everyone OK with that? Lunch here on Wednesday?'

There was a general murmur of agreement. Natalie nodded, pleased with the outcome. That left just one other point she needed to make, and she wasted no time. As they left the dining room she drew Harry to one side, her fingers digging into his arm.

'For God's sake,' she said in a low voice, 'will you try to be a bit more understanding with your wife?'

He looked at her mutinously. 'She's being thoroughly unreasonable, Nat. Why the hell she agreed to come here if all she's going to do is hide upstairs, I don't know.'

Natalie stared at him in amazement. 'Are you telling me—?' she began.

'Telling you what?'

'Do you really not know, Harry?'

'Know *what*, for pity's sake?'

Natalie's hand dropped from his arm. 'She's *pregnant*, you oaf!' she said.

SIX

Kent

With the Bournemouth visit cancelled, or rather – as Sophie was quick to emphasize – postponed, Mark was after all able to spend time with his daughter before she started school, time which he treasured despite his wife's prickly attitude. The gulf between them seemed to be widening, and he was at a loss to know what to do about it. Florence, meanwhile, had taken to 'big school' like a duck to water, and bombarded him on his return each evening with a detailed account of all she'd been doing.

No further reference had been made to Peter's lapse and Mark hadn't seen him since, though Sophie had occasionally driven Florence down after school to have tea with her grandparents. Summer slid into autumn, and he was busier at work as sales became brisker after the summer dip.

It was in the middle of September that an unlooked-for complication arose. Mark had always kept his social and business lives separate, but at the last office Christmas party Sophie had met the wife of one of his colleagues and they'd become friends, meeting several times for lunch. There was therefore little he could do when they received an invitation to have dinner with the Lesters at their home in nearby Petts Wood.

To add to Mark's reluctance, Simon Lester wasn't someone he'd have chosen to spend out-of-office time with. Conventionally good looking with dark, curly hair and blue eyes, he made a practice of flirting with every woman in sight, confident they'd welcome his advances and impervious to the odd brush-off. A more personal irritation was his habit of invading people's space, invariably coming uncomfortably close when speaking, so that Mark continually found himself having to take a step backwards.

Still, he told himself, an off-the-cuff dinner invitation, even though it would have to be returned, needn't make them bosom buddies. If the wives wished to continue meeting, fine, but he'd no intention of committing to a regular exchange of visits.

It was therefore with resignation rather than anticipation that he set off that evening, following sat nav directions to a substantial detached house in a leafy road. The gates stood open and he drove in, parking alongside a BMW on the gravelled drive.

Their ring on the doorbell was answered almost at once. Simon opened the door with a flourish, kissing a somewhat startled Sophie on the lips before slapping Mark's shoulder.

'Don't take your coat off, mate. I thought we'd nip down to the local for a swift half before dinner.'

'I haven't greeted our hostess yet,' Mark pointed out a little stiffly, handing over a bottle of wine in its brightly coloured holder.

'Good of you, Mark – thanks. Jen!' he shouted over his shoulder. 'Chop, chop! Our guests are here!'

Jenny came hurrying out of the kitchen and Mark, who'd no recollection of her from the office party, was aware of surprise. He'd expected Simon's wife to be the height of glamour, but the woman whose hand he was shaking wasn't even pretty. She wore little makeup and her dark hair was tucked behind her ears like an overgrown schoolgirl. Her smile, though, lit up her rather plain face, making him ashamed of his shallow assessment.

'I'm so pleased to meet you,' she was saying. 'I've heard a lot about you from Sophie.'

It would be interesting, Mark thought drily, to know exactly *what* she'd heard.

'Eating at eight thirty, right?' Simon cut in. 'We'll be back by then.' And allowing no time for further exchanges, he shepherded Mark back outside.

'Do we need to do this?' he protested as Simon unlocked the BMW. 'I'd be just as happy to—'

'Gives the girls a chance to have a chat while they settle the kids,' Simon responded, and before Mark had even buckled his seatbelt, he reversed quickly out on to the road.

* * *

The visit to the pub did nothing to improve Mark's opinion of his host. No sooner had they sat down with their glasses than he embarked on a string of criticism of the Bellingham's directors, some of which bordered on slander, before moving on to crude comments about the female staff.

'God knows how she got the job,' he remarked of one of them. 'Probably slept with old Taylor.'

Mark, acutely uncomfortable, made several attempts to deflect the conversation and eventually, having met with no success, ended the flow by saying firmly, 'Well, it's the weekend so let's forget about work, shall we? Where did you get to on holiday this year?'

Simon flung him an assessing glance, then smiled reluctantly. 'In other words, shut it! Fair enough.' He drained his glass. 'Ready for another?'

'Not for me, thanks.'

'Hang on, then, while I get a top-up.'

Mark watched him as he elbowed his way confidently to the bar, slapping the odd man on the back as he went. It was, he thought wryly, going to be a long evening.

'Well, you *were* in a mood, weren't you?' Sophie began as soon as the car door was closed. 'God knows what they thought of you.'

'I'd no chance to be in any mood,' he returned steadily. 'You and Simon kept the conversation going non-stop.'

'Don't tell me you were jealous!'

Jealous, no, but annoyed, most certainly. Simon, virtually ignoring his wife, had bombarded Sophie with extravagant compliments throughout the meal and she'd played up to him quite shamelessly. In an attempt to redress the balance, he'd begun a quiet conversation with Jenny – though, to give her her due, she seemed unfazed by her husband's behaviour. No doubt she was used to it.

'Anyway,' Sophie went on, without waiting for a reply, 'Simon's good fun, and a little harmless flirtation doesn't hurt anyone.'

She was probably right, he conceded silently; had it been anyone else it would no doubt have washed over him, but he'd allowed his dislike of Lester to colour the evening. Oh well, one down, one to go, but there was a point on which he was adamant: when the return visit took place there would be no nipping down to the pub; pre-dinner drinks would be served at home.

In the weeks that followed, it was borne in on Mark that their brief social contact had convinced Simon they were close friends. At work he constantly sought his opinion or advice, came to sit at his table at lunch and even, when Mark was unable to avoid him, joined him on the train home, all of which added to a deepening resentment, compounded by the fact that he was unable to do anything about it.

It was about a month after the return dinner that he began to notice a change in Simon. He'd developed an air of suppressed excitement that was vaguely disturbing, and on one occasion arrived late for a meeting, with the unconvincing excuse that it hadn't been in his diary.

Had Mark been more kindly disposed towards him he might have enquired if anything was wrong, but he'd no intention of encouraging further intimacies. His resolve was reinforced when, as they were passing each other in a corridor one day, Simon said quickly, 'Should either Jen or Sophie ask, I'm working late tonight, OK?'

He'd disappeared round a corner before Mark could reply. So that was it! Bloody fool! he thought, and promptly dismissed the matter. But it soon became clear he was not, after all, to be allowed to remain uninvolved.

It was around this time that Sophie met James Meredith. Stella, meanwhile, had continued her association with Lance, which had developed into a full-blown affair about which she regaled Sophie over weekly cups of coffee. As a result Sophie had become increasingly bored with what she considered her own humdrum existence, and increasingly envious of her friend's illicit romance.

Ten days before their proposed half-term holiday, Stella phoned to invite Sophie to join her and Lance for a meal. 'He's bringing a friend, so you needn't feel awkward,' she added. 'Tell Mark it's a girls' night out – and it is, in a way.'

Sophie hesitated. Eager though she was to meet the glamorous Lance, the implication that his friend was almost certainly male added the dimension of risk, and unease mingled with her rising excitement.

'There's no way he'll find out,' Stella urged. 'The restaurant's in Beckenham, and no one we know ever goes there. Come on, Sophie, you're always saying life is dull – here's a chance to spice it up a bit!'

'Who is this friend?' Sophie asked, still cautious. 'Have you met him?'

'No; his name's James Meredith. Fortyish, divorced. That's all I know, but Lance says he's great. Heavens above, it's only a meal! If you don't like him, you need never see him again.'

But suppose she did like him? Sophie thought tremulously. Was she embarking on something she would find it difficult to withdraw from? Though as Stella pointed out, it *was* just a meal. No lines need be crossed. She drew a deep breath. 'OK,' she said. 'Thanks – I'll come.'

Following the practice of previous, more innocent, girls' nights out, Stella called for her in her bright red Mazda, but on this occasion drove only the short distance to the railway station, where she parked. Immediately a Jaguar farther down the line flashed its lights and she gave a breathless little laugh.

'Right. Change of transport. Out we get.'

Heart in mouth, Sophie followed her across the car park, and as they approached two men emerged from the Jag. It wasn't possible in the sporadic lighting to form much impression, but Stella, having reached up to kiss the taller of the two, stepped back and said brightly, 'Lance, this is Sophie. Sophie, meet Lance, and . . .'

'James,' said the other figure, holding out a hand to each in turn. 'Hello, Stella, I've heard a lot about you. Hi, Sophie.' Having released her hand, he opened the back door of the car and motioned her to get inside. Heart beating high in her throat, she did so.

It was a twenty-minute drive to Beckenham, and during the journey Sophie was intensely aware of the man at her side. So far, all she knew of him was that he had a pleasant speaking voice although, disconcertingly, he made no attempt to talk to her and the two of them sat in almost total silence while Stella and Lance chatted in the front, occasionally tossing the odd comment over their shoulders to their back seat passengers.

God, what was she doing? she thought in sudden panic. She shouldn't have come – of course she shouldn't! Unconsciously she stiffened, her fingers tightening on her clutch bag, and gave a little gasp as a hand was laid over hers.

'Relax!' James said softly, and squeezed it before removing his own. She was more than thankful when, minutes later, they drew into a small car park behind the restaurant and she was able to escape his proximity.

Only when they took their seats was Sophie afforded her first clear look at their escorts, and it was immediately obvious that Lance was the better looking; his dark hair was slightly overlong and his eyes an unfathomable brown, leading her to wonder if he'd Spanish or Italian blood in his ancestry.

James, less striking, had grey eyes and his hair was a nondescript brown but, paradoxically, of the two men it was he who held the attention. There was something compelling about his lean, deeply grooved face and the grey eyes were at the same time watchful and assessing. Sophie guessed that while Lance was adept at the social graces, you had to take James as you found him. She felt a little quiver, which she instantly stifled, and quickly picked up the menu.

The cuisine was Italian, and some of the initial awkwardness melted as they discussed the various dishes on offer. Stella and Lance, who'd obviously been here before, were able to advise on some of the lesser-known choices, and Sophie, following their recommendation, enjoyed a delicious pasta dish she'd not come across before.

As the wine continued to flow, she belatedly pulled herself together. God, what was wrong with her? Heaven knew, she was used to socializing, meeting people, making small talk; what was it about this man that rang such loud alarm bells?

Shaking off the last of her reserve, she took full part in the conversation, relating stories about Florence and her first days at school that made everyone laugh. It wasn't until they were back in the car that apprehension returned. James hadn't addressed her directly over the meal, and she wondered if they'd again sit in silence on the homeward journey. To try to forestall the possibility she made some comment as they set off, but when he only nodded in reply she gave up the attempt and instead tried without success to establish why this enigmatic man should attract her so strongly, when she so obviously didn't interest him.

Well, she thought philosophically, she'd soon be home and need never see him again. One thing was certain: in future she'd deflect all Stella's attempts to fix her up with a blind date.

She was therefore totally unprepared when, as they were nearing Chislehurst, he suddenly pulled her against him and began to kiss her, deeply and passionately, ignoring her frantic attempts to free herself until, with a little moan, she gave up.

She was scarcely aware of the car slowing down until the lights of the station appeared ahead and Lance turned into the car park. James released her abruptly and she sat up, gasping for breath and pulling up the neckline of her dress. In the front seat, Lance and Stella were locked in a goodnight kiss.

Sophie scrabbled for the door handle and as she half-fell out of the car the October night struck cold, snatching what little breath she had. James had also climbed out, but only to take his place in the front passenger seat.

'We'll wait till you're safely in your car,' Lance said, and their headlights were a welcome guide as they stumbled towards the dark shape of the waiting Mazda. Then they were inside, and with a farewell toot, the Jaguar sped off.

'Well!' Stella said. 'What did you think of him?'

Sophie had barely recovered her breath. 'I'll tell you when I've had time to decide,' she said, and Stella gave a low laugh.

The hall clock was striking half past eleven as Sophie locked the front door behind her. The sitting room light was off and she guessed Mark had gone upstairs. Glancing in the hall mirror, she rubbed the smeared lipstick from around her mouth and gave a little shudder. James's kisses had aroused her and she was still trembling.

Like an old woman she pulled herself upstairs by means of

the banister and, from habit, glanced into Florence's room. As usual the little girl had thrown off the duvet, and Sophie crept in and replaced it gently round her shoulders. Then she went on to their room, where Mark was sitting up in bed reading.

He glanced up. 'Had a good time? You're later than I expected.'

'It was quite a drive to the restaurant,' she said, starting immediately to undress.

'It was just you and Stella?'

'No, a couple of her friends came along, It was a good evening.'

She went into the en suite and stood for a minute staring into the mirror at her flushed face and wide eyes before beginning mechanically to wash and brush her teeth, her mind replaying those few intense minutes in the car. Then she returned to the bedroom, crept into bed and, gently taking Mark's book out of his hand, whispered, 'Make love to me.'

Margot said over dinner, 'Lydia's still worried about Peter.'

Charles took a drink of wine. 'So am I.'

'She's convinced he's seriously ill but afraid to go to the doctor. She keeps pleading with him, but he refuses point-blank.' She paused. 'Did you ever speak to him about that business at the party?'

'Yes, but he was pretty evasive, stuck to the story that it was a combination of sunstroke and champagne.'

Margot shook her head. 'I could have accepted that – just – if the after-effects hadn't gone on so long, but it's been nearly two months. Lyddie says he's lost weight and is not eating or sleeping well.' She looked across at her husband. 'Come to that, *you're* not eating or sleeping as well as usual. Don't tell me it's catching!'

Charles shrugged dismissively. 'Unlike Peter, I could do with losing a bit of weight.'

'I thought we might invite them to dinner. Try to shake him out of whatever's bothering him.'

'Good idea.'

That settled, she went on to recount a telephone call she'd received that morning from Delia, but Charles was barely listening. He'd more reason than Margot to worry about his friend: the other day in the office, Peter had said suddenly, 'If anything happens to me, you'll take care of Lyddie, won't you, Chas?'

'Nothing's going to happen to you!' he'd retorted sharply.

'But if it did?' Peter persisted.

'Then of course we would. You don't have to ask.'

And that had seemed to satisfy him. Yes, Margot was right: it would be good to have the pair of them here, as they'd been so many times in the past and would, he told himself firmly, be again.

Towards the end of the month the school broke up for half-term, and despite Mark's continuing annoyance Sophie and Florence left to spend the week with Stella in Bournemouth. Not, he admitted, that he'd have had much time to spend with his daughter if they'd stayed at home; a big auction was coming up and there was a lot of preparation to see to. His parents had invited him for Sunday lunch, but for the rest he was snatching ready meals out of the freezer when he got home and eating them in front of the television, frequently falling asleep over them.

So he'd no convincing excuse when, as he was about to leave the office, Simon, who knew Sophie was away, suggested a meal in town.

'I'm not much company at the moment,' he prevaricated. 'I'd probably fall asleep mid-sentence!'

'The same goes for me, but there's something I want to discuss with you.'

Mark's heart sank still further. 'Can't we do it here?' he asked without much hope.

'No way. No booze, for a start. There's that new steak house round the corner; we could give it a try.'

The thought of a plate of steak and chips rather than the frozen lasagne awaiting him swung the balance. 'OK, then,' he said.

It wasn't long, though, before Mark regretted being so easily swayed. No sooner had they given their order than Simon leaned confidentially across the table.

'Strictly *entre nous*,' he began in a low voice, 'have you ever – you know – strayed from the fold?'

Mark frowned. 'What?'

'You know, had the odd dalliance. Since you've been married, I mean?'

'No, I have not,' Mark said emphatically.

'Well, if I were married to Sophie, I probably wouldn't have, either!'

As he was still leaning forward, Mark added reluctantly, 'Why, have you?' As if he didn't know the answer!

'Well, since we're being honest, then, yes I have, on the odd occasion. Nothing serious, just to pep things up a bit. With the best will in the world, Jen, bless her, is a bit strait-laced.'

'Simon, I really don't think I want to hear—'

'Please!' Simon laid an impulsive hand on his arm, removing it almost at once as their food arrived. They sat silently while it was laid before them, confirmed that they would prefer English mustard, and waited while it was brought. Then Simon continued as though there'd been no interruption.

'The hell of it is, though,' he went on in a low voice, 'this time it's a case of the biter bit.'

'I don't follow,' Mark said stonily, picking up his knife and fork.

'I've fallen in love, mate. Good and proper.'

'Then you'd better fall out again.'

Simon smiled, shaking his head. 'Trouble is, this is the real thing, and she feels the same. God, why didn't we meet years ago?'

'I don't quite see why you're telling me this.'

'Because I want your advice, mate. You've met Jen; what do you think would be the best way to approach her?'

Mark laid down his fork and stared at him disbelievingly. 'You're not trying to tell me you're thinking of leaving Jenny and the kids? For God's sake, man, come to your senses! You probably thought it was "the real thing" during your other "dalliances", as you call them. This will pass, like the others did.'

Simon shook his head again. 'Not this time. I can't let her go – it's as simple as that.'

'What's simple is that you asked for my advice, and I'm giving it to you. Forget this woman, whoever she is, and give your family the love and attention they deserve.'

'You wouldn't say that if you knew who she was,' Simon said a little sulkily, spearing a chip.

'I don't care who the hell she is, she's off-limits and you know it.'

'I expected a bit of understanding, if nothing else.'

'Then you've come to the wrong person. Jenny's sweet and amusing and generous, and she doesn't deserve this.'

'God, you sound like her father! I *know* she doesn't deserve it, but I can't go on living a lie.'

'Try!' Mark said harshly. 'It's better than breaking up your marriage.'

'She'd want me to be happy. If she knew how I felt, she wouldn't stand in my way.'

'And have you spared a thought for what it would do to her? To the children?'

'You're talking as though I'd cut them off without a penny! Of course I'd make every provision for them. They could stay in the house—'

'Big deal!' Mark drew a deep breath. 'Look, I'm sorry if you thought I'd be an easy ride, tell you that you were doing the right thing. Since I've no intention of doing so, we'd better talk of something else before we both get indigestion. Subject closed, OK?'

Simon's face was mutinous. There was a pause, then he said in a low voice, 'OK. Forget I said anything.'

'With pleasure,' Mark replied.

Despite himself, however, over the next few days Mark's thoughts kept returning to Simon's unwelcome confidences. What had he meant about Mark understanding if he knew who the woman was? Could it be someone he knew personally, or – highly unlikely – some minor 'celebrity', a term now seeming to encompass anyone who'd appeared, however fleetingly, on television?

Well, he told himself, no matter who it was, his advice

would have been the same. He could only hope Simon would take it.

The weather in Bournemouth was disappointingly cold and blustery, and despite their mothers' urging, the little girls showed no enthusiasm for walks along the front. Consequently by the end of the week they'd visited a considerable number of attractions including the aquarium, a theme park and a ride on the land train, and were beginning to run out of ideas.

On the Thursday evening Stella, who'd been exchanging daily texts with Lance, hurried into the kitchen where Sophie was cooking their meal.

'Guess what!' she exclaimed excitedly. 'Lance is suggesting he and James come down and join us tomorrow evening!'

Sophie felt a tide of heat sweep over her. 'They can't stay here!' she said sharply.

'No, of course they can't; they'll book in at a B and B. I think we deserve a bit of "us" time, don't you, after trailing dutifully after our kids all week?' She studied her friend's face. 'You did like James, didn't you? You never really said.'

Sophie hesitated. 'To be honest, I couldn't make him out; he virtually ignored me all that evening, and then—'

'Leapt on you in the car? Yes, I noticed! But he obviously likes you, or he wouldn't have agreed to come.'

'They *are* coming, then?'

'Yes, driving down after work. Obviously we can't go out, so I've suggested they come here for a meal.'

Sophie was trying to ignore her accelerated heartbeats. 'Suppose one of the children wakes?'

'Well, they haven't so far, but we'll face it if we have to.'

Sophie was floundering around searching for objections. 'We can't see them during the day. Florence tells Mark everything she does in meticulous detail.'

Stella smiled. 'They're not worried about the daytime – they'll amuse themselves playing golf, walking, whatever – but we'll have two lovely long evenings with them. Come on, Sophie, it'll be great! I don't know about you, but I'm getting withdrawal symptoms!'

'You promise they won't spend the night here?'

'Not the night, no, and if you and James want to spend the evenings watching TV, feel free. Lance and I will find another way of amusing ourselves!'

By the following evening Sophie was in a state of panic. Suppose the children didn't go straight to sleep and wandered back into the living room? Suppose she and James found nothing to say to each other?

'Relax,' Stella told her. 'Lance will text to check the coast's clear this end. If it isn't, they'll wait till it is. Everything will be fine.'

As it happened the children did go straight to sleep, tired out by the strenuous day their mothers had intentionally planned, and at eight thirty a discreet knock on the door heralded their visitors. Sophie had wondered if James would match the picture of him that had haunted her for the last two weeks, hoping desperately that her response to him would have moderated in the meantime. But when he appeared in the doorway, the memory of his mouth and hands surged over her and she knew she was lost.

Somehow she managed to eat the food Stella had prepared, helped down by several glasses of wine. It was a leisurely meal; no one seemed in a hurry for it to end, and to Sophie's consternation it was she who was impatient for the next stage of the evening.

Eventually the coffee was finished and everyone helped carry the dishes through to the kitchen. Then Lance took Stella's hand, said to James, 'See you in about an hour,' and disappeared with her into her bedroom, closing the door softly behind him.

Sophie, who'd been putting away the napkins, froze. The time she'd been both dreading and longing for was upon her. Almost fearfully she turned, to find James surveying her quizzically, one eyebrow raised.

'Well?' he said. 'Shall we follow suit?'

She could only nod in reply.

The next morning while Stella was preparing breakfast the children wandered into the kitchen in their pyjamas. There was no sign of Sophie.

'Where's Mummy?' she asked Florence.

'She's got a headache,' the child answered, climbing on to her chair and reaching for her juice.

Stella made no comment, but having settled them with their milk and cereal, she went to Sophie's door and tapped gently. There was no reply, but she didn't wait for one. The curtains were still drawn and Sophie was lying face down on the bed, clutching the pillow with both hands.

'Sophie?'

She turned over slowly, shielding her eyes from the faint light in the room. Her face, Stella noted with shock, was red and swollen from crying. She hurried over and sat down on the bed. 'Sophie, what is it? What's wrong?'

'I can't believe what happened last night,' she said in a clogged voice. 'I've never behaved like that in my life.'

'He didn't hurt you, did he?' Stella asked sharply.

Sophie shook her head. 'He wasn't exactly gentle, but he didn't hurt me. But God, Stella, I barely know him! What was I thinking of? He hardly said a word the whole time, and at the end he just got up, dressed, nodded to me and went out to meet Lance. How do you think that made me feel?'

Stella reached for her hand. 'Would you rather I cancelled this evening?' she asked tentatively, and felt Sophie's hand tremble in hers.

After a minute she replied in a low voice. 'No. Now do you understand why I hate myself?'

Sophie did not appear to have benefited from her holiday, Mark thought when he greeted her and Florence on their return that Sunday. She was pale and unusually subdued, and her explanation of a headache came as a surprise, since she so rarely suffered from them.

'Don't bother unpacking, then,' he told her. 'Sit down and relax. I'll bath Florence and give her her tea.'

She nodded apathetically and when, after taking her case upstairs, he glanced into the sitting room, she was leaning back against the sofa with her eyes closed and what looked suspiciously like a tear on her cheek.

He hesitated, unsure what to do, but Florence was calling

him from the kitchen and there was no time for any in-depth conversation, if that was what was required. Somewhat uneasily, he set about cooking some pasta.

Half an hour later, when he paused at the sitting room door on their way upstairs, she was in the same position and he presumed she was asleep.

'Don't disturb Mummy,' he whispered. 'She'll come and say goodnight when you're in bed.'

Florence at least was her usual chatty self, endlessly regaling him with accounts of their activities in Bournemouth. She looked a picture, Mark thought fondly, with her hair pinned up for her bath and her little face glowing.

'And this morning we went for a last walk along the beach and Uncle Lance bought me and Rosie an ice cream and—'

She broke off, flushing, and Mark's attention, which had started to wander, snapped back. *Uncle Lance?*

'What is it, sweetie?'

Florence's lip trembled. 'Mummy said not to tell you,' she said. 'It's our secret.'

Mark felt a tide of anger well up inside him. Was it possible this was the cause of Sophie's malaise? Who the hell was 'Uncle Lance', and why was he a secret? It seemed that not only was his wife seeing another man, she was involving their daughter. Downstairs he heard the house phone begin to ring. Well, she could damn well wake up and answer it. He was busy. But he'd have a word or two to say to her later.

'Daddy?' Florence's worried little face looked up at him. 'Mummy won't be cross, will she?'

He pulled himself together. 'Of course she won't, darling.'

Behind him he heard the bathroom door open, and Florence's eyes went past him. Talk of the devil, he thought. He turned, ready with a sarcastic remark, but stopped short at the sight of his wife. If she'd been pale before, she was now chalky white and leaning for support against the door frame. God, perhaps she was really ill!

He got clumsily to his feet. 'Sophie?' he said sharply.

Her eyes, huge and clouded, moved slowly towards him and came into focus. She moistened her lips. 'Could you . . .?' she began, and swayed against the door frame.

Mark glanced back at the child, aware of her alarm. 'It's all right, sweetie – I shan't be a minute. Play with your toys.'

He moved swiftly forward, took Sophie's arm and moved her outside, closing the door behind him.

'Tell me,' he said urgently.

Her eyelids were fluttering and he was afraid she was going to pass out. Then her fingers fastened on his arm, digging into the flesh. 'Margot just phoned,' she said, her voice halfway between a croak and a whisper. 'Mum asked her to.' She drew a deep, shuddering breath. 'Daddy's just died!'

SEVEN

Drumlee

Harry stood staring after Natalie as she followed the others into the sitting room. *Pregnant?* She couldn't be! She'd have said! Anyway, they'd not discussed starting a family since they were first married; Jess had always stressed the importance of her career and he hadn't wanted to press her.

Sudden coldness washed over him. *Suppose she was planning to get rid of it?* Was that why she hadn't told him? Or was Nat wrong? OK, she was a medic, but she wasn't infallible. Another thought: since *she'd* noticed, had anyone else? Was he the only one who hadn't spotted the signs? Surely Seb would have said something? A *baby*? He felt foolish, angry and elated, all at the same time.

He drew a deep breath. If Jess was upstairs he'd go straight up and tackle her about it. However, glancing into the sitting room, he could see her sitting on the sofa, apparently perfectly composed, with a glass of water on the little table in front of her. So it would have to wait till bedtime.

He came slowly into the room, looking at his wife with new eyes. *Was* there anything different about her? She didn't seem to have put on weight. What other signs should he look for? Across the room he caught Natalie's eye and she gave an almost imperceptible nod. He walked over and sat beside Jess. She was in the middle of a conversation with his mother and barely seemed to register him. Well, he'd get her full attention later, he promised himself, and, taking the cup of coffee handed him, prepared to bide his time.

'I hope everyone remembers,' Natalie was saying, 'that not only is Tuesday Mum and Dad's big day, it's also Valentine's Day!'

'In other words,' Douglas remarked with a smile, 'any

"unknown admirers" had better make damn sure they post
their cards tomorrow!'

God! Mark thought, why hadn't Helena warned him? They
could have bought a card in town yesterday. He'd assumed
Valentines were a thing of the past now Sophie had left, but
remembered with a sudden tug of guilt that he'd always sent
a card to Florence – something he'd omitted this year. Would
one posted tomorrow reach Dormers by Tuesday? He could
only hope so.

Jessica stood up, smoothing her skirt. 'Would you excuse
me if I go up now? I've had a headache threatening ever since
bowls; an early night and some paracetamol should stop it in
its tracks.'

'Of course, dear,' Paula sympathized. 'I hope it lifts soon.'

Damn! Harry thought. It was only just after nine – too early
for him to follow her – and ten to one by the time he got upstairs
she'd be asleep. It looked as though the discussion now weighing
heavily on his mind would have to wait till the morning.

Up in their room, Nick said, 'I don't know how you feel, but
it occurred to me that as the two not-quite family members
we should make some contribution towards the anniversary. I
mean, Nat has bought something, obviously, and no doubt so
has Helena, but they're not really from *us*.'

'Good idea,' Mark agreed. 'Anything in mind?'

'Perhaps a bouquet of red roses, to be delivered before they
go to lunch?'

'Perfect!'

'Right; no doubt we'll be going out some time tomorrow,
so I'll arrange it then.'

Mark nodded, taking off his tie. 'Let me know what I owe
you.'

Natalie came back from the bathroom to find Helena tapping
on her mobile.

'Whoever are you texting this time of night?' she asked.

'A work colleague,' Helena said shortly.

'God, you businesswomen! It's Sunday night, for Pete's
sake!'

Helena flushed. 'She'd left a message earlier that I've only just picked up.'

'And it couldn't wait till morning?'

'Is it really any of your business?' Helena flared.

'No, I suppose not.' Natalie shrugged off her dressing gown and climbed into bed. Though she wisely held her peace, she remembered now that her sister had been on her mobile at the leisure centre. Either Helena's job was considerably more frenetic than she'd thought, or she wasn't telling the truth. Knowing her sister, Natalie concluded it was the latter.

Sebastian lay awake a long time that night, listening to Danny's soft snuffles in the darkness. The call from Diana had unsettled him more than he'd realized, and now that he'd nothing to distract him memories came flooding back of their time together.

God, how he'd loved her! They'd met at university; she'd been his first love, and, for a long time after she left, he'd feared she would also be his last. But now there was Miriam, Diana's complete opposite, whom, as he'd told Harry, he was on the verge of loving. But, as he'd also told Harry, there were complications, and he had to weigh up whether or not they could be resolved without causing hurt to Danny.

He turned over impatiently, trying to focus on his current problem, but the image of Diana again intruded – Diana with her sleek hair, her long legs, her indefinable air of elegance no matter what she wore. Diana who, so in control of herself, had nevertheless responded to his lovemaking with a passion that had surprised and delighted him and which, remembering it, made him want her again with an urgency he was unable to gratify.

He sat up abruptly, reaching for a glass of water and managing to locate it without turning on the light. A cold bath would be more appropriate, he thought with grim humour as the icy liquid went down his throat, and he wondered yet again if there'd been any stage at which, if he'd acted differently, things might not have ended as they did. But he'd been so sure of the stability of their marriage that he'd not seen the danger latent in the quiet, unassuming presence of Gordon

Carrington, who'd insinuated himself into their circle without his noticing and proceeded, apparently without effort, to steal his wife away from him.

He realized belatedly that he was still holding the cold water glass and that not only was his hand numb, but the freezing air in the room was insidiously chilling his neck and shoulders. Swearing softly he lay down again, pulled the duvet up to his ears and, condemning his ex-wife to perdition, made a concerted effort to go to sleep.

When Jessica stirred and opened her eyes the next morning, Harry was sitting on a chair in his dressing gown. She stretched luxuriously, reminding him of a cat.

'Been awake long?' she asked sleepily.

'Most of the night.'

She frowned, propping herself on one elbow. 'Oh, bad luck. Was it something you ate?'

'No.' He gazed at her steadily, at her tangled hair and her face flushed from sleep, and felt a lurch of love for her. He took a deep breath and blurted out, 'Are you pregnant?'

Her eyes widened and she gave a little gasp. 'Where did that come from?'

'Natalie thinks you are. Is it true?'

A hand went to her mouth. 'Oh, Harry!' she whispered, and burst into tears.

He was with her instantly, gathering her into his arms and holding her closely. 'Oh, my love,' he said against her hair, 'why didn't you tell me?'

She shook her head blindly, sobbing into his chest.

'I know it wasn't planned,' he went on when she didn't speak. 'But we always wanted a family some time, didn't we? Were you afraid I wasn't ready?'

She moved back slightly, reaching under the pillow for a handkerchief. 'No,' she said unsteadily, 'it was more selfish than that; it was because *I'm* not.'

'But why, sweetheart? We've both got good jobs and a lovely home. Surely there's no need to wait any longer?'

'But don't you see?' she burst out. 'It's *because* I've a good job – and one that I love. There are important contracts that

I've been nursing for months and they'll need all my care and attention to land them, but lately I've not been able to concentrate because I've felt so *rotten*! This weekend, for instance, I haven't dared go out or come to meals, because I keep being sick! I only just managed yesterday to get back from bowls in time. Goodness knows what everyone thinks of me!'

He felt a wave of shame at his own intolerance. 'But surely there's something you can take for the sickness? Have you been to the doctor?'

'No.' Her voice was muffled.

'Why ever not?'

She looked up at him with swimming eyes. 'Because that would make it – official.'

'But you are sure? It is definite?'

She sighed. 'Oh, it's definite all right. I've done several tests and they all showed positive.'

'Well, we'll ask Nat to write a prescription for the sickness and track down a pharmacy. As for these contracts, how long do you need to complete them?'

She shrugged and blew her nose. 'Six to eight weeks, I suppose.'

'Well, once you're over the sickness you'll be perfectly capable of dealing with them, won't you? The baby won't be here for – what? – seven or eight *months*?'

'I suppose so,' she said dubiously. 'As long as I do stop vomiting.'

'And when the baby's born,' he went on encouragingly, 'Joanna can carry on for a while without you. You're always saying she's your right hand. Then, when you're ready to go back, we'll find a nanny.'

He cupped her face between his hands. 'So the only thing left to establish, now all the problems have been sorted, is whether or not you want this baby. Do you, Jess?'

She looked at him for a long moment and all her doubts fell away. 'I don't deserve you, Harry Crawford,' she said humbly.

He smiled, feeling his heart begin to lift. 'Be that as it may, you've not answered the question. Do you want this baby?'

She drew a deep breath. 'Yes,' she said. 'Of course I do.'

The news of Jessica's pregnancy lightened what was a dismally dark and wet day, but when approached, Natalie regretfully shook her head.

'You'd have to get a prescription from your own doctor,' she told her, 'but by all means have a word with the local pharmacist, who should be able to advise you. In the meantime stick to small meals of bland food – I'm sure Meg and Andy will oblige – and take plenty of drinks of tea or water. A biscuit before getting up in the morning should help, too – some people swear by ginger nuts.' She looked more closely at her sister-in-law. 'Incidentally, you look fine to me. Have you been sick this morning?'

'Oh!' Jessica gazed at her in belated realization. 'No – no, I haven't, actually.'

'Then you might be over it. Just go carefully this week, and see your doctor as soon as you get home. And congratulations, Jess! It'll be great to have a baby in the family.'

Slowly the day passed. They were all in for lunch, but afterwards, as the rain had lessened, they went for a brisk walk, peeling off in twos and threes en route. Mark took the chance to slip into a stationer's and buy a card for Helena. The choice was pretty limited and he'd no idea whether to go for a humorous or a sentimental one. Since their alleged engagement was so recent, he gritted his teeth and went for the latter, then bought a jokey one for Florence, scribbled a message inside it and posted it in a nearby pillar box. Fingers crossed it would arrive in time.

By the time they set out that evening the rain had moved on and a clear sky promised frost later. It had been arranged that they'd meet the Mackays at a restaurant in town rather than the hotel. 'It's where we go when we've a night off and want to escape!' Blair had explained. A phone call ascertained there'd be a choice of dishes suitable for Jessica, and as she'd been well all day she was prepared to take the risk.

The restaurant was warm and welcoming after the chill outside. Since they were a large party a round table had been laid for them upstairs, and they had the room to themselves. The Mackays were already there, and there was a flurry of greetings among those who'd not already met on this visit. Mark and Nick were introduced to Ailsa and her French husband, a small man with fair, thinning hair, and they took their places round the table.

Mark was agreeably surprised at the scope of the menu, and the prices were a fraction of what he'd expect to pay at home. There was a general discussion as Blair and Ailsa recommended various dishes they'd enjoyed on previous visits, and the orders were finally given. The waiter departed and there was a brief lull in the conversation, broken by Ailsa saying, 'Oh, by the way, did your mother get her phone call?'

The Crawfords looked blank. 'What phone call?'

'Someone rang the hotel on Thursday wanting to speak to her. I told them she was at Touchstone and they said they had that number.'

'We didn't arrive till Friday, so we wouldn't know,' Seb replied. 'Though I can't think who'd be calling her up here.'

'They didn't leave a name,' Ailsa said.

'Speaking of your parents, is your father still working full-time?' Blair enquired. 'He must be nearing retirement, surely?'

'He has a couple of years to go,' Helena said, 'though I think he'll stay on as long as he can. He's a workaholic, and I don't envy Mum having him under her feet all day! He'll be like a caged tiger!'

'Dad's slowing down a bit now,' Ailsa remarked. 'He's letting Blair take over more and more.'

Mark, who could take no part in this conversation, sat back and studied the speakers in turn. Ailsa, a slim, petite blonde seated diagonally to his left, was attractive rather than pretty, with a retroussé nose and a ready smile. He imagined she'd be ideal in a front-of-house position, either at the hotel or at the tourist board where she worked, quick to put people at their ease.

Blair too had the ease of manner requisite to his line of work, and Mark decided on further acquaintance that he must have imagined the tension he'd thought he detected at their earlier meeting. Certainly he was now the life and soul of the party, lightly flirting with both Jessica and Natalie who sat on either side of him.

As well as himself and Nick, both newcomers, there was another member of the party who was taking little part in the general chat – Jean-Luc, the French chef. Mark guessed this was partly because he'd not met the Crawfords before and felt overwhelmed by them – a totally understandable reaction – but also, as became evident, because his English was somewhat limited. Mark, who'd had some dealings with French colleagues, made an effort to draw him into the conversation and was rewarded by a flood of hard-to-follow French. He did, however, gather that he'd been in the UK for just over two years, and that he and Ailsa had married the previous autumn.

Ailsa, flashing Mark a grateful smile, joined in the conversation, unobtrusively translating when the flood of Gallic became too swift. Once his shyness was dispelled and he was able to converse in his own language, Jean-Luc proved to be an interesting companion, with unexpected flashes of humour.

After several minutes of this *entente cordiale*, Helena, who was sitting on Mark's other side, reclaimed his attention.

'Hey, lover boy – remember me?' she demanded, only halfjoking. He saw to his surprise that she was a little drunk.

'How could I forget you?' he parried, and to his startled embarrassment she leaned over and kissed him on the lips.

'That's better,' she said, to a brief round of applause, and Mark, his face uncomfortably hot, hastily returned to his steak, his mind buzzing with hitherto unconsidered questions.

The rest of the meal passed without incident and as the wine flowed he and Nick played more part in the conversation. When asked about his work, Mark had to remind himself not to be too explicit; in the unlikely event of anyone asking for him at Bellingham's, the auction house would deny all knowledge of Adam Ryder.

By the time they left the restaurant to go their separate ways, the Merlin contingent crossing the square to the hotel and the Touchstone party starting up the hill towards home, it was almost eleven thirty and the ground was white with frost.

Jessica, who'd partaken of only a small amount of the bland dish prepared for her, was looking tired, but there had been no return of her sickness and good reason to believe it had run its course.

Seb went ahead of them up the garden path and opened the front door with his key. The hall light was on, but the sitting room was in darkness and it was clear Paula and Douglas had retired to bed. Mark had turned towards the stairs when Helena caught hold of his arm.

'You two go on up,' she told Natalie and Nick, her voice slightly slurred. 'We'll join you later.' And she gently pushed him towards the sitting room.

Alarm bells started to ring: this was not what had been agreed between them, and he had no wish to take advantage of her when she was in a vulnerable state. He drew back and she gave a low laugh, giving him an extra nudge.

'I won't eat you!' she said and, pushing the door closed with one foot, she put her arms round him and started to kiss him. Her breath tasted of wine and he felt his own quicken. Gently he took hold of her arms and pulled them away.

'This isn't part of the deal,' he said. 'You're a little tipsy and you'll regret this in the morning.'

'According to the Bible, the morrow can take care of itself. Anyway, Benton's rules don't apply here – we're free agents. And as a "free agent"' – she made quotation marks in the air – 'I want you to make love to me.' And as, nonplussed, he continue to stare at her, she added softly, 'Please!'

Mark's head swam. He too had imbibed fairly freely during the meal. She hadn't switched the light on and the room was lit only by the dying fire. When he didn't speak, she took hold of his hand and led him towards it. Then, as its warmth stole over their cold bodies, she systematically began to kiss him, while her fingers fumbled at the buttons of his shirt.

His breath caught in his throat. He'd not been with anyone since Sophie left – nor, for that matter, with her for a consid-erable time before that – and here was an undeniably attractive woman literally begging him to make love to her. Why the hell was he hesitating?

The last of his resistance dissolved and with mounting urgency he pulled her down on the rug.

When he finally reached his room, Nick was sitting up in bed reading. Embarrassed, Mark avoided meeting his eye.

'Sorry about that,' he muttered.

'Don't be!' Nick replied, and Mark heard the grin in his voice. 'You did us a favour – Nat and I took advantage of your joint absence!'

'That's all right then!' he replied.

Later, lying in bed, Mark reflected with a touch of shame that although he had wholeheartedly enjoyed Helena's lovemaking, he was still not sure whether or not he actually liked her.

EIGHT

Kent

Mark stared at her, his mouth suddenly dry. *'What?'*
Sophie crumpled against him and he caught her, holding her up.

'I don't know any details,' she whispered, 'only that Mum needs me. Now.'

'Of course.' He took a deep breath, feverishly searching for words of comfort that wouldn't come. *Don't worry? It'll be all right? It could be worse?* The normal platitudes were useless in the face of such enormity.

He took her arm and gently led her into their bedroom, where the suitcase from Bournemouth stood waiting to be unpacked. 'Lie down for a minute, darling, you've had a shock. I'll get Florence out of the bath, then I'll throw a few things together and take your case back down. We can be there within the hour.'

She murmured something he didn't catch and he paused in the doorway.

'What did you say?'

'I said it's my fault,' she repeated tonelessly.

'That's nonsense, sweetheart! How can it possibly be your fault?'

'I'm being punished,' she whispered.

Mark stared at her – nonplussed. She was in shock but he hadn't time to reassure her – he'd left Florence for long enough. With a heavy heart he returned to the bathroom, where his daughter was playing unconcernedly with her toys.

'Mummy's had some bad news, sweetie,' he began. 'Grandpa Peter's . . . very ill, so we're going down to be with Granny.'

He lifted her slippery little body out of the bath and wrapped her in a towel. 'So we'll put your day clothes on again and you must be a good girl, because Mummy's very upset.'

Her eyes filled with tears. 'Will Grandpa be all right?' she asked tremulously.

Mark hesitated. God help him, he'd no idea how to prepare a child for such news. Should he delay the full facts, let her acclimatize to a lesser fear?

'I don't know, darling,' he hedged. 'We'll have to wait and see.'

She was silent for a moment, sitting on his knee and submitting to the drying process. Then she said, 'Would it help if I drew him one of my pictures?'

Mark hugged her fiercely. 'I'm sure it would,' he said.

It wasn't until they were in the car that Sophie told him her mother was at his parents' house. 'I don't know why,' she said dully, and retreated back into herself.

The journey down was a nightmare. Sophie barely said a word, sitting in frozen silence beside him, hugging herself and staring straight ahead. From time to time he glanced in the mirror to check on Florence, who was gazing out of the window at a world turned suddenly upside down. He tried to think of something comforting, but without success. Eventually, in desperation, he slid one of her CDs in the slot and the car was filled with the wildly inappropriate jollity of 'Chitty Chitty Bang Bang'. At least it filled the silence.

Belatedly he wondered if he should have phoned his mother to learn what he could before their arrival, but it was too late now. *Peter was dead!* The words kept repeating themselves in his head but he could make no sense of them. Could Sophie have misunderstood, got the message wrong, suspected the worst when the news was really less dramatic – a fall, perhaps? Even a heart attack?

Then, suddenly, they were turning into his parents' gateway, and he wished there were a dozen more miles before he had to face what lay ahead. The car had barely come to a halt before Sophie fumbled frantically at her seatbelt and half-fell out, running crookedly to the front door which opened as she reached it. Mark could see his mother outlined against the hall light, but Sophie pushed past her, intent on reaching Lydia.

With a heavy heart he climbed out himself, freed Florence

from her car seat and carried her into the house. Margot, white-faced, was still in the doorway.

'Mum . . .' he began, and came to a halt.

She nodded and took the child from him. 'Go after her,' she said. 'I'll take care of Florence.'

Lydia was standing by the fire in the sitting room, clutching Sophie to her. Over her daughter's head she caught sight of him and stretched out an arm. He went to her, murmuring her name, but could think of nothing else to say. She enfolded him in her embrace and for several long minutes the three of them stood unmoving. Tears, he thought, would come later; at the moment shock was dominant.

Then Lydia drew a deep breath and released them. 'You both need a drink,' she said steadily. 'I'm sure Charles will do the necessary.'

His father! Mark realized with a stab of guilt that it was the first time he'd thought of him. It would be an enormous shock for the old man; he and Peter had been friends almost since boyhood. He said quickly, 'I'll go and find him,' and hurried from the room.

Margot was coming down the stairs.

'Florence?' he queried.

'Totally exhausted, bless her – the drive back from Bournemouth, then this. I tucked her into bed and she was asleep before I'd reached the door.'

He nodded. 'Tell me what happened.'

'I'll get us a drink,' she said, and he followed her into the kitchen.

She poured them both a neat whisky and he joined her at the table, scene of so many family meals. Her face was drawn, her eyes red-rimmed, and Mark reached impulsively for her hand. She smiled bleakly, returning the pressure.

'The first I knew was a completely hysterical call from Lydia mid-morning.'

Mark stiffened. '*Mid-morning?* Why in heaven's name didn't you phone then? Granted, Sophie wouldn't have been home, but I could have broken the news when she got back.'

Margot shrugged helplessly. 'What could I have told you? All I could make out was that Peter was dead, and we assumed it was a heart attack. So we dashed over, and were appalled to find the place crawling with police.'

'*Police?*' He seemed unable to stop repeating what she said. 'For God's sake, why?'

Margot drew a steadying breath. 'Mark, I could hardly tell Sophie on the phone, but he . . . he hanged himself.'

Mark's world tilted. 'He . . .?'

'They're treating it as a crime scene. *Crime!* Can you believe it? The drive was so full of vehicles we'd difficulty parking – ambulance, forensic van, a couple of police cars . . . Honestly, Mark, it was like stumbling on to a TV set. A uniformed policeman was at the door, and wouldn't let us in until Lydia came flying out and hurled herself into my arms.'

She took a gulp of her whisky. 'The staircase was sealed off with that ghastly yellow tape.'

Mark drained his own glass. 'Where did—?'

'In his bathroom, from the shower curtain rail.' Margot automatically refilled his glass. 'Lyddie says she called up to tell him his coffee was ready, and when he didn't come she went to look for him. He'd locked himself in the bathroom and there was a note on the floor outside, telling her to call the police.'

'My God!' Mark paused. 'Did it say why he'd done it?'

'No, she said it was just full of apologies and saying how much he loved her. I've not seen it myself – the police took it, which added to her distress. But what possible reason *could* he have had? He'd no money worries, and he and Lyddie adored each other.'

'You thought he wasn't well, though, didn't you? Perhaps he'd found out he'd an incurable illness or something.'

Margot shrugged. 'Anyway, they interviewed her for hours and she told them she'd been worried about him but it had never entered her head he'd do anything like this. They wanted to know if there'd been any other deaths in the family, or if he'd tried to kill himself before. When they finally finished with her and the doctor had been, I asked if we could bring her home with us. Obviously she couldn't stay there, with the house full of police and the upstairs sealed off, so they made a note of our address and we came back. That was when I phoned you – really the first chance I'd had.' She ran a hand over her face. 'It's going to be so dreadful for her; there'll have to be a post-mortem and an inquest, which will bring it all back.'

After a minute Mark said, 'She seems remarkably calm now.'

Margot nodded. 'The doctor gave her something. God help her when it wears off.'

'That reminds me, I said I'd take Sophie a drink.' He got to his feet. 'Where's Dad?'

'He shut himself in the bedroom as soon as we got back. I *know* he's grieving, but he might spare a thought for the rest of us. Perhaps you'd have a word with him.' She pulled herself to her feet. 'Go on up and I'll see to Sophie's drink.'

Mark finished his second glass, and with a heavy heart went up to his parents' bedroom. His knock on the door produced no response. He knocked again, called softly, 'Dad?' and, in the continuing silence, turned the knob and opened the door.

Charles was standing at the window, his back to the room and his hands driven deep into his pockets. He didn't turn as his son came in.

'Dad, it's Mark. Can I . . . get you anything?'

No response. Cautiously Mark walked over to him and took his arm. 'I'm so sorry, Dad,' he said.

Charles turned his head, and Mark was shocked by his ravaged face and the tracks of drying tears on his cheeks. He'd aged ten years since he'd last seen him.

'Why the hell did he do it, Mark?' he demanded, his voice cracking. 'God knows, there was no need for that!'

Mark frowned, puzzled by the choice of words. 'How do you mean, no need?'

Charles shook his head, making a dismissive gesture with one hand, but Mark, suddenly suspicious, studied him more closely.

'Do you know something?' he demanded. 'Something that might explain it?'

Charles stared at him for a moment, and Mark had the odd feeling that it wasn't himself he was seeing. Then he shook his head and said brusquely, 'No, of course I don't.'

'But you were his closest friend,' Mark persisted. 'If he was this desperate, surely you'd have known?'

Charles ran a hand through his hair. 'Peter could be very secretive when it suited him.'

'Really?' Mark gave a half laugh. 'I'd have said he was the most open person I knew!'

'Then you'd have been wrong.' Charles drew a deep breath. 'How's Sophie?'

Mark hesitated, reluctant to let the subject drop, but it seemed his father was not to be drawn further. 'Numb, I think is the best description. And in need of a drink, which is why I came to find you.'

'No one else capable of pouring one?'

'We need you downstairs, Dad,' Mark said quietly. 'We all do.'

Charles met his eye and slowly nodded. 'Let's go down, then.'

It was without doubt the worst evening Mark could remember. Though by then it was after eleven and they were all exhausted, no one suggested going to bed. For varying reasons none of them had had much to eat that day, but they weren't hungry and Margot's offer of food was declined. Nonetheless, she prepared a plate of small, triangular sandwiches and a few of them were absentmindedly eaten.

Lydia was seated next to Sophie, holding tightly to her hand as though afraid that by letting go she might lose her grip on everything. She'd emerged from her frozen state, though not sufficiently to allow the relief of tears; instead, she obsessively went over the events of the day – her last conversation with Peter at breakfast, the light-heartedness with which she'd been planning the week ahead.

'And last night we were talking about going away for Christmas. He never gave any *sign* . . .' She broke off, unable to finish the sentence, and Sophie reached blindly for a handkerchief.

'How could I not have known?' Lydia ended piteously – the same question Mark had put to his father. Had Peter really been as secretive as Charles maintained, or had the urge to end everything come on him suddenly, and he'd put it into effect without further thought? Charles himself had barely spoken since he'd joined them. He sat slightly apart from the group, gazing into the fire and nursing a whisky glass which he periodically refilled.

During one of the lulls in conversation, Mark said apologetically, 'I'm sorry to bring this up, but I shall have to go in to work tomorrow. We've a big auction coming up and there's really no way I can delegate—'

'Of course, dear—' Margot began, but Lydia broke in almost hysterically.

'You're not taking Sophie away?'

He hesitated, but Sophie said quickly, 'No, of course not, Mum. I'll stay for as long as you need me. Mark, will you phone the school and let them know Florence won't be in next week?'

A house full of grief would not, he felt, be the best place for his daughter, but he'd no alternative to offer.

'Of course,' he said.

'And you'll be back tomorrow evening?' Margot pressed. 'You should be with the family at a time like this, not alone in an empty house. When you go in tomorrow, love, take a case with what you'll need for the rest of the week, then you can catch the Sevenoaks train from work. Text me once you're on it, and I'll come and meet you.'

Mark, too tired to argue, nodded. If he were based here at least he'd see Florence, whom he'd missed during her week in Bournemouth. And, of course, Sophie, he added mentally, appalled that it had come as an afterthought.

'Now that's settled,' Margot said firmly, 'I think we should all go to bed. Lyddie darling, you have the pills the doctor gave you?'

Lydia nodded. 'Only enough for three nights. I'll need more than that.'

'At a time like this, it's easy to become addicted to them,' Margot warned.

Lydia shrugged, turning to her daughter. 'Will you sleep in my room tonight, darling? I don't want to be alone.'

'Of course I will,' Sophie said.

Later, as Mark was undressing in his old bedroom, he remembered he'd never asked her about the mysterious Uncle Lance, and as things now stood, he probably wouldn't get the chance again. He could only hope it wasn't important.

Mark slept only fitfully, his mind a kaleidoscope of images of the day: Florence, rosy-faced in her bath before the bombshell; his father's devastated face; and Sophie almost impatiently pushing him away as he tried to comfort her. 'I must go to Mum,' she'd said. Most haunting of all was an imagined vision of Peter, the jovial, generous figure who'd been so much a part of his life, hanging lifeless from the shower rail.

And echoing beneath all these snatches was Charles's odd comment: *There was no need for that.* What exactly had he meant?

It was borne in on Mark, not for the first time, how little he knew his father. During his and Jonathan's childhood he'd not been the kind who read bedtime stories or played football with them, and it was their mother who came to their infant nativity plays and, later, cheered them on at sports day. 'Daddy's at work' had been the constant refrain, and their father's study at home was strictly out of bounds. It struck Mark that his hands-on love for Florence was in part a determination to be different, to play an active role in his daughter's life.

While he accepted that many men felt awkward with children, as their sons grew older a deep male companionship often developed. In their case it had not. Perhaps Charles had left it too late to unbend, to show belated interest in his sons' accomplishments. Well, Mark told himself, it was his loss, but it did mean that at times of crisis there was no bond to draw them together.

The household was still asleep when he left at seven the next morning. The flashbacks to his childhood had brought his brother to mind, and it occurred to him that in all probability he'd not been told the news. Therefore, as he started the car and drove slowly out of his parents' drive, he plugged in his hands-free mobile and clicked on his number.

It rang for several minutes before Jonathan's sleepy voice reached him. 'What the hell, Mark? Do you know what time it is?'

'Time you were awake on a Monday morning,' he replied.

'The alarm goes at half past; you've robbed me of a precious thirty minutes.' There was a brief pause, then his voice strengthened. 'So what is it? Must be something serious at this hour.'

'I'm afraid it is, Jon.' Mark took a deep breath. This would be the first time he'd voiced the words that had dominated the last twelve hours. 'It's Peter – Peter Kingsley. There's no easy way to say this: he's hanged himself, Jon.'

Silence. Then a strangled, *'What?'*

Mark turned on to the main road, joining a stream of traffic, and went on doggedly: 'Mum phoned us yesterday evening and we drove straight down. Lydia was at the parents', because Dormers was full of police and forensic teams.'

'My *God*!' Then, *'Police?'*

'They're treating it as a crime scene, God knows why. I've left Sophie and Florence down there but I'm in the car now on the way to work.'

'But why, Mark? Why in heaven's name would he do a thing like that! God, poor Lydia!'

'Yes.'

'Look, we can't really talk now. If you're going in to work, could we meet for lunch? I need to know all the details, to try to make sense of it.'

'Lunch would be great, Jon. Twelve thirty at the Dominion?'

'See you there,' Jonathan said and rang off, leaving his brother feeling marginally better as he continued his drive home.

Delia was still beneath the bedclothes.

'Who the hell was that?' she asked sleepily. 'I hope they'd a good reason for calling at this ungodly hour.'

Jonathan walked slowly to the window and stared out at the gradually lightening sky. 'Yes, as it happens, they – or rather he – had.'

She sat up, glancing at the clock on the table beside her. 'Couldn't it have waited till you got to the office?'

'It wasn't work, Delia, it was Mark.'

She paused in the act of pushing back her hair. 'Mark? Whatever did he want?'

'Very bad news, I'm afraid.' Jonathan turned to face her. 'It's hard to believe, but it seems Peter Kingsley hanged himself yesterday.'

She gasped, her hands flying to her face as the colour drained out of it. 'God, *no!*' she whispered. 'Oh, please, *no!*'

Jonathan stared at her, dumbstruck. This was not the reaction he'd expected. He went to her and tried to pull her into his arms, but she struggled to free herself. 'Darling, what is it? Whatever's wrong? I mean, I know it's ghastly, but you hardly knew him.'

She looked at him wildly. 'Are you sure? Could there be a mistake?'

'No, Mark and Sophie went down last night. She and Florence are still there.'

She stiffened suddenly as though a thought had struck her. 'Oh *God*, he didn't leave a note, did he?' Her fingers clenched his arm.

'I don't know. I'm meeting Mark for lunch, and I'll learn more then. But I don't understand why you're so upset.'

She stared at him a moment longer, then she turned abruptly and flung herself face down on the bed, pummelling the pillow with both hands.

Jonathan gazed at her in total incomprehension. This, he thought feelingly, he could do without. Though Peter had always been a part of his life, to his knowledge Delia had met him only twice – at their wedding in June and at the birthday party two months later.

The memory of that party pierced the shield of his grief. Something had been wrong then – Peter's unaccustomed tipsiness, his breakdown back at the house. Had that been the beginning of his troubles, or were they already well advanced?

Suddenly impatient with his wife's excessive reaction, he said briskly, 'Come on, darling, pull yourself together. It's time we got ready for work.'

And as she still lay unmoving, he left her and went for a reviving shower.

NINE

Drumlee

'You can put the light on,' Natalie said.

Helena had paused in the doorway, outlined by the landing light behind her. 'So you're still awake,' she commented.

'Uh-huh. You're not the only one who's been enjoying yourself! Well done, by the way, for seizing the opportunity.'

Helena pressed the switch and the room leapt into blinding clarity. 'A pleasure,' she said.

Natalie studied her curiously; there was definitely something different about her – she'd noticed it as soon as they arrived – something she couldn't put a finger on. But then Helena had always been uniquely herself, unfathomable to the rest of them.

Watching her undress, she amused herself by pondering how, if her sister had come into her consulting room, she would have assessed her, and was surprised by the qualifications that followed each appraisal. Self-confident, but with an underlying hesitancy; decisive, though sometimes backtracking; opinionated, yet occasionally contradicting herself. Will the real Helena Crawford please stand up? she thought fancifully. It was amazing, she reflected, that her sister, with all these inconsistencies, should be so competent and highly thought of at work.

Without intending to, she said suddenly, 'You do love him, don't you? Adam?'

Helena glanced at her in surprise. 'Of course. To quote Prince Charles, "whatever love means".'

'Not a very happy analogy.'

Helena shrugged, slipping her nightdress over her head. 'Go to sleep,' she said.

But it was almost an hour before Natalie was able to obey her. Following her earlier musings, her mind slipped back over her relationship with her sister – the four-year-old and her frequent tantrums, the tale-telling, the teenage slights and betrayals. One of her less endearing habits had been to flirt openly with the local boys, irrespective of whether they had girlfriends, and when they'd broken off relationships and were her devoted slaves, drop them and move on to the next one. Natalie suspected Blair Mackay had been a case in point.

Since they'd left home and their lives had separated she'd lost track of her sister's love life, though when they *had* met there was always a different man in tow. 'I have a low boredom threshold,' she'd said once, when Natalie had challenged her on the subject.

Admittedly Jack had lasted longer than the others. It had really seemed he might be the one, and when they split up it was several weeks before Helena could bring herself to tell her family. She'd seemed really devastated, yet they'd barely had time to adjust to the break-up before Adam was paraded in front of them. Did he know what he was letting himself in for? Natalie wondered; they'd been together for only a matter of weeks. He seemed a decent man and didn't deserve to have his heart broken on a whim of her sister's.

She sighed and turned over. Across the room, Helena's breathing was slow and regular. Not a care in the world! Natalie thought drowsily, and at last drifted into sleep.

Valentine's Day, and as was only to be expected everyone received a card, even young Danny – from his mother. Harry, watching Seb open his, presumed it was from Miriam and was glad for him, while Mark reflected that in view of last night's shenanigans it was probably as well he'd gone for the romantic option. He was still having difficulty in accepting that that hour in front of the fire had actually taken place.

Paula and Douglas had booked a taxi to take them for a *déjeuner à deux* at the café where they'd shared their first meal together all those years ago, and since they wouldn't be needing the car, Seb suggested the rest of them should drive out of town, see a bit of the countryside and find somewhere for lunch. The problem of numbers was solved by Harry and Jessica opting out; she didn't want to risk travel sickness and Harry decreed she should rest before the evening's celebrations.

It had been decided that the present-opening ceremony would be held at midday, and the bouquet of red roses was delivered just as it was about to begin, to be greeted with surprised delight. Mark, who would never have thought of it, flashed Nick a look of gratitude.

Among the family's gifts were Helena's ruby glass vase; a pair of engraved champagne flutes from Harry and Jessica; a bottle of vintage red wine together with a copy of *The Times* from the day of their wedding from Sebastian; and from Natalie a card enclosing a page torn from a gardening catalogue showing a Japanese maple with deep red leaves which, she explained, would be delivered once they were back home. Douglas had presented his wife with a ruby ring, while her present to him was a watch – alas, not, as she laughingly apologized, studded with rubies.

Then their taxi arrived and bore them off for their lunch and the others piled into Douglas's car, Nick beside Seb in the front, Mark and the two sisters in the back, with Danny perched on Natalie's knee. It was a bright sunny day with a strong wind and Seb took the coastal road, affording them the view on one side of steep cliffs, sweeping beaches and sunlight glinting off white-flecked waves, and on the other side lush farmland stretching away towards distant hills.

At one point he parked at the side of the road and they got out, buffeted by the strong wind, to walk along the cliffs overlooking a beach of golden sand.

'The sea looks pretty rough,' Natalie commented, turning up the collar of her jacket. 'Very different from how we're used to seeing it. I remember picnics in this bay, and looking for shrimps in the rock pools.'

Back in the car, Sebastian drove for another twenty minutes before pulling in to a whitewashed café on the cliffs that boasted the best seafood for miles around. Their appetites stimulated by their stiff walk, they didn't dispute the claim, appreciating both the excellent food and the cosy atmosphere of the little café with its draped fishing nets and lobster pots.

When he'd woken that morning Mark had been apprehensive

of meeting Helena after their impromptu lovemaking but, unable to detect any change in her attitude, assumed she regarded it merely as an extension of the charade they'd embarked on. He'd found himself wondering, with a frisson he tried to suppress, whether it would be repeated on their return from the celebrations that evening.

However, during the drive and the meal that followed it she'd become noticeably more tense, taking less and less part in the conversation, her mind apparently elsewhere.

'Everything OK?' he asked her in a low voice, under cover of the general chat.

She glanced at him with a slight frown. 'Yes, why?'

'You just seem a bit . . . distracted.'

She raised an eyebrow. 'Not paying you enough attention, lover boy?'

He flushed and she gave a low laugh.

'Only teasing.'

Danny clamoured for her attention, and the moment passed.

On the return journey Nick ceded his front seat to Mark, who, still slightly ill at ease with Helena, was glad to take it. He'd not so far had a one-to-one conversation with Sebastian and found, slightly to his surprise, that they had several interests in common, concluding with mild regret that were he really who he purported to be, they could have become good friends.

A taxi arrived at seven thirty to convey everyone to the Merlin and they emerged from their various rooms to gather in the hall. To Mark's relief there was no sign of dinner jackets, the men simply in suits and ties. Since he hadn't brought even a suit with him (his holiday wardrobe not being geared for formality) he'd opted for the blazer he'd worn each evening, and fortunately this seemed to pass muster.

The women, however, had dressed for the occasion and were in various styles of evening wear. Natalie, with her hair piled on top of her head, was in coffee lace and Helena wore an ankle-length dress in sea-green that complimented the red-bronze of her hair. Danny, much to his disgust, was to be left in the care of Meg and Andy, the caterers, and was still protesting he should be allowed to go with them.

'It'll be far too late and not your kind of food at all, kiddo,' Sebastian assured him, ruffling his hair. 'You wouldn't enjoy it, but I'll bring you back a piece of cake.'

And with that he had to be satisfied.

The Mackays had invited them for drinks before the meal in their private apartment, and the express lift bore them swiftly upwards, opening on to a carpeted hallway where Callum and Lexie were waiting to greet them. They were ushered into a large, comfortable-looking sitting room where a fire burned in a handsome stone grate and a bottle of champagne stood waiting in an ice bucket.

Mark hadn't met Callum Mackay before, but liked him immediately. He was tall and broad-shouldered, with sandy hair and grey eyes edged with laughter lines. He shook hands with both Mark and Nick, offering congratulations on their respective engagements, though Nick and Natalie's had still to be formally announced.

Although the French chef would be otherwise engaged Mark had expected Blair and Ailsa to be present, and saw both Helena and Natalie look quickly around, registering their absence. Their glances were intercepted by Lexie.

'Ailsa and Blair hope you'll excuse them,' she apologized, 'but they send their congratulations and best wishes.'

She handed Paula a gaily wrapped parcel. 'With our love,' she said, and Paula opened it to reveal a china plate with a view of Drumlee and the dates *1977–2018*. 'Not,' she added, 'the date of your wedding, but of your meeting here the year before.'

Paula gave both her and Callum a hug, tears in her eyes. 'That's lovely!' she exclaimed. 'As you know, Drumlee has always been very special to us.'

Douglas kissed Lexie and shook Callum's hand. 'It will hang in a place of honour!' he said.

The champagne was poured and toasts made and the four eldest members of the party reminisced over the years they'd known each other, one memory leading to another and most of them evoking laughter. Eventually an internal phone rang and Callum, having answered it, announced that their table was ready. More hugs and thanks were exchanged and the Touchstone party re-entered the waiting lift.

'I do think Ailsa and Blair might have made the effort,' Helena remarked as they descended.

'Oh, I don't know,' Paula answered comfortably. 'After all, it's their parents we've been friends with all these years.'

'But we've been here for a lot of those years, and so have they.'

'Hey!' Douglas interposed jovially. 'Whose anniversary is it?'

There was no time for more as the lift door opened and the maître d' met them and escorted them to their table.

The fact that it was Valentine's Day obviously outweighed its being out of season, because the restaurant was full and a buzz of conversation filled the air. They'd been allotted a table in an alcove with a window overlooking the floodlit square and its magnificent display of snowdrops, and as though to accentuate their perfection, during the evening a few flakes of snow began to fall.

'Suppose it comes on heavily and we're snowed in at Touchstone?' Harry joked. 'We'd have to stay here till the thaw!'

'An unlikely scenario,' responded Sebastian.

'But possible!' Harry insisted. 'Planes grounded because of ice on the wings. It *is* February in Scotland, after all! As long as there were no power cuts, it would be rather fun!'

Mark inwardly agreed with him – he'd have no problem with putting his life on hold at the moment; he still hadn't come to terms with his father's incredible confession, and on top of that there was Simon's hysterical and as yet unexplained phone call which he supposed he'd have to deal with.

They'd spent the previous Thursday valuing items at a country house in Dorset which had necessitated an overnight stay, and against his better judgement he'd been cajoled into promising that, should anyone enquire, he'd confirm that he and Simon had spent the evening together – which was patently untrue.

Back at the hotel he'd phoned his assistant and emailed him

his valuation report, then, welcoming the prospect of a relaxing evening, ordered room service, had a bath and was watching television in his pyjamas when, to his extreme consternation, he received a call from Jenny.

'Hi, Mark,' she'd begun. 'Sorry to trouble you, but Simon's phone's gone to voicemail. Is he with you?'

Mark closed his eyes, cursing himself for the extracted promise. 'Not at this precise moment, Jen, he's in the gents'. Shall I ask him to call you?'

'Oh!' She gave a little laugh. 'No, on second thoughts, don't bother – I only wanted a chat and he'll be home tomorrow anyway. Thanks, Mark.' And she rang off.

Well, he'd done his duty, he'd told himself grimly, and, deciding on an early night, had gone to bed. Which was why, when Simon's late call, gabbled and incoherent, woke him from a deep sleep, he'd given him short shrift, assuming he was drunk, and simply put the phone down.

The following morning he'd left early, anxious to get home, pack and leave again in time to catch the York train. Simon's call had completely slipped his mind. Perhaps he should check it had been nothing important.

He was roused from his musings by the ceremonious arrival of a bottle of champagne and an impressive cake decorated with red ribbon and appropriate lettering scrolled in red icing. Douglas and Paula cut it together, Harry took a photograph with his phone and the waiter, having filled their glasses, bore the cake away to be cut into portions – an unwelcome reminder for Mark of Peter's ill-fated birthday party.

Sebastian tapped on the side of his glass to claim everyone's attention. 'I won't stand up since we're in a public room,' he said, 'but I would like to propose a toast to our parents, congratulating them on reaching the big four-o and wishing them many more happy years together. So please raise your glasses to Mum and Dad, or, in the case of Jessica, Nick and Adam, to Douglas and Paula!'

They all complied, and when their voices had died down Douglas tapped his own glass. 'Thank you all for your good wishes and the magnificent presents we've received. I may say this is the perfect way to spend our anniversary, in the place where we first met and with the whole family around us. And of course I must also add sincere thanks to your mother for putting up with me for so long!'

There was laughter and a smattering of applause and he raised his glass. 'So let's drink to the family!' he proposed, and they duly did so. By the time the waiter returned with slices of cake, to be washed down with the last of the champagne, the evening was winding down, and as the other tables began to empty, the maître d' approached to murmur discreetly to Douglas that their taxis had arrived.

It had stopped snowing but a light coating, reminiscent of the cake's icing, lay over pavements and hedgerows, lending a touch of magic to the night. Mark was no longer expecting a repeat of Helena's advances; though she had smiled and laughed when required, a part of her seemed detached from them all, and he was curious to know what was troubling her. He'd no chance to ask her; as soon as they reached home they wished each other goodnight and went to their rooms.

'Oh well,' Nick said philosophically as he closed their door, 'I suppose it was too much to hope for!'

And Mark, with a rueful smile, agreed.

The clock in the hall chimed twice, its clear notes sounding through the silent house. Paula, still wide awake, sighed in frustration. It had been a full day, what with the present-opening, the romantic lunch *à deux* and the evening's celebrations, and by rights she should be ready to sleep, but her mind was still spinning. The constant looking back that the day had triggered now brought to mind other details of that momentous holiday with her parents and younger brother: the boat trips, the beach picnics, the nightly dances at the hotel where, 'across a crowded room' as the song had it, she'd caught her first glimpse of the man she'd marry.

It was no good, she thought impatiently; sleep was a long way off. She'd go downstairs and make herself a hot drink. Carefully, so as not to wake her gently snoring husband, she slid out of bed and pulled on the thick dressing gown she'd had the presence of mind to bring with her. As she opened the bedroom door the air struck chill and she repressed a shiver. The three other doors were firmly shut and there was no sound other than the loudly clicking clock. Holding up her dressing gown, she went slowly and cautiously down the stairs.

A faint glow came through the fanlight over the front door, lighting her way along the passage to the kitchen. She took milk out of the fridge, poured it into a pan, reached down a tin of chocolate powder. Then, having made her drink, she returned along the passage to the sitting room. Meg and Andy had spent the evening here and there was still a residue of warmth coming from the ashes in the grate. She pulled up a chair, sat back with the hot mug between her hands and let the memories come.

Douglas had been holidaying with two other students and after that first evening, when he asked her to dance and his companions had each selected a partner, the six of them spent every day together, driving to different beaches squeezed into an open-topped sports car, visiting shows on the pier, but mostly sunbathing, swimming and dancing. And almost before she knew it, Paula had fallen in love.

Her parents, who had believed it to be a holiday romance, became increasingly concerned when, after they returned home, Douglas continued to write and telephone, driving over to see her whenever his university course allowed.

'You're both much too young,' they insisted. 'Once he's graduated he'll have to find a job and will have enough trouble supporting himself, let alone a wife! If you're convinced he's the one, what's the harm in waiting? You can both build up your finances and if in a couple of years you're still sure of each other, then go ahead and marry.'

Now, for the first time, Paula wondered whether, if they'd followed that advice, they would still have been together. But he was her first love, she his first serious relationship, and both had been convinced they'd live happily ever after.

They hadn't, of course. Oh, it had been fine for a while; they were both working, so the only time they spent together was in the evenings and at weekends, and it was like an extended honeymoon. But then Seb was born, and disturbed nights led to tiredness and shortness of tempers, not helped by the sudden reduction in their income. The arguments and bickering began, and at one point she'd actually packed her bag and taken the baby back to her parents for a couple of months before giving in to Douglas's pleadings to return home. Not that she'd been blameless in all this. Looking back, she could see she'd often been selfish, intent on having her own way and not pulling her weight when things went wrong.

Then, of course, the other children began to arrive and she'd immersed herself in caring for them, becoming more mother than wife, as Douglas frequently complained, leading to further arguments and accusations.

Nevertheless, it had been a shock when, as they were going through a particularly rocky patch, Douglas suddenly decided to opt out and applied for a year's transfer to London, knowing that for various reasons, including not wishing to interrupt the children's schooling at a crucial stage, she wouldn't accompany him.

She had believed that was the end of their marriage, and any thought of celebrating their ruby wedding would have seemed moonshine. But yet again, probably taking more than his share of blame, Douglas had persuaded her to allow him back into her life. Incredibly, that was nearly twenty years ago, and it had been a wake-up call. After a shaky start when they'd tiptoed around on eggshells, their lives had realigned and, caught up in the highs and lows of everyday living, they'd evolved into a normal middle-aged couple, happy enough with each other's company. Sadly, however, though deeply fond of him, she'd never recaptured that first unquestioning love.

She drew a deep breath, aware that she'd come full circle, and as the present reasserted itself, remembered with a jolt that something was troubling him, something he'd so far refused to discuss. Once they were back home she must get to the bottom of it. She stretched and, glancing into her mug, saw it was empty. Time to return to bed.

It was while Nick was having a shower the next morning that Mark remembered his intention of checking on Simon and, taking his phone out of the drawer where he'd left it that first evening, he switched it on. To his astonishment he was immediately confronted with a long list of missed calls – three, as he'd half-expected, from Simon, but one from another work colleague – unusual while on leave – and, potentially more worrying, one from Lydia and no fewer than four from his mother, the latest timed at seven o'clock the previous evening.

Florence! he thought instantly, his heart racing. God, don't let anything have happened to her! He glanced uncertainly at the bedroom door, not knowing how long Nick would be, and aware that any conversation he might be having on his return could compromise his identity. Shrugging on his windcheater, he ran quickly downstairs and out of the front door.

Last night's snow, thinly spread though it was, had frozen and lay glittering in silver crystals on the lawn. He opened the gate and walked a few quick steps along the pavement until the hedge screened him from the windows of the house. Then, his heart thumping uncomfortably, he clicked on his mother's latest call and her voice rang out on the still winter air.

'Mark, where *are* you? We're going out of our *minds* with worry! The police think you might know where she is – she disappeared the day you left, after all, and was seen catching the London train. We had to admit we'd been unable to contact you, and to make matters worse, you'd said you'd be walking in the York area but the B and Bs in the vicinity deny all knowledge of you. In view of all this, added to your estrangement, you can see why they're becoming suspicious. If, God forbid, anything's happened to her, you'll be the number one suspect! We just need to know you're both safe, Mark, so *switch on your phone* and call us!'

TEN

Kent

'So go through it again,' Jonathan directed, grinding black pepper over his steak. 'The first you knew of it was when Sophie appeared at the bathroom door?'

Mark nodded. 'I'd heard the phone, but I was bathing Florence so left it for her to answer. Then the door opened and she was just standing there, white as a sheet and leaning against the jamb. I scrambled to my feet and hurried outside, pulling the door shut behind me. And . . . then she told me.'

'Poor little Soph,' Jonathan said softly. 'What exactly did she say?'

'That it was Mum on the phone, and she'd told her her father had died.'

'Not that he'd hanged himself?'

Mark shook his head, looking at the plate of food in front of him and wondering if he'd be able to eat it. 'She shut me out, Jon; I wanted to comfort her, but she only wanted her mother.'

Jonathan glanced at him. 'I suppose that's natural enough,' he said uncertainly. He cleared his throat. 'Actually, I had rather a weird reaction from Delia. When I told her, she seemed to go into shock for a minute, then flung herself face down on the bed.'

Mark frowned. 'But she didn't know him, did she?'

'No, that's just the point. She'd only met him twice. God knows what got into her.'

'Intimations of mortality?'

'Hardly. God, Mark, she's a hard-headed businesswoman, not given to the vapours. I can't think what came over her, and she wouldn't explain.' He paused. 'She asked if he'd left a note?'

'Yes, the police took it, but Lydia said it was only apologizing and saying how much he loved her.'

'No clue there, then.'

'No. I've been thinking of that party . . .'

Jonathan nodded. 'Me too. Something was certainly up then. That was the last time I saw him.' He shook his head. 'I just can't get my head round it. Peter, of all people.'

'I know.'

'You're going back this evening?'

'Yes, for as long as Sophie and Florence are there.'

'I don't envy you, in the circumstances.'

'I admit I'm not looking forward to it. Dad's very shaken too, as you might imagine, and I can't think it's good for Florence to be surrounded by so much grief.'

'I suppose there'll have to be an inquest?'

'And a post-mortem,' Mark said grimly. 'It'll probably be the end of the month before we can hold the funeral, by which time it'll be almost Christmas. And Lord knows what'll happen then.'

'Delia's parents have invited us to theirs this year. I suppose from now on it'll be turn and turn about. At least you've never had that problem, with the Kingsleys having always been part of our family Christmas.'

'Which will make it even harder this year.'

Jonathan nodded soberly. He glanced at his brother's untouched plate. 'Are you going to eat that or just sit looking at it?'

Mark sighed, picking up his knife and fork. 'I'm really not hungry.'

'You need to keep your strength up.'

'So who else will be at the Firths' for Christmas?' he asked, reluctantly starting to eat.

'Just her parents and brother, I think. A very select party after the crowd I'm used to.'

'But you get on with them OK, don't you?'

'To be honest I hardly know them, with their living down in Devon. Her brother works in London, though, and he's been over a couple of times for a meal.'

'He's gay, isn't he?'

Jonathan nodded. 'But not in a relationship or anything. Seems a decent bloke, and he and Dee are very close. I think she feels protective of him, being the elder sister.'

'Well, I'd willingly swap your Christmas for mine this year,' Mark observed feelingly.

'If I write a note to Lydia, will you take it down for me?'

'Sure.'

'And let me know when the funeral is. Obviously we'll be there; I just hope Delia doesn't repeat this morning's performance; it would be highly embarrassing.'

Mark was grateful to have his work to concentrate on that day, but Simon was waiting for him when it was time to go home.

'Thought we could have a chat on the train,' he said, falling into step beside Mark.

'Afraid not, I'm catching the Sevenoaks one. Family bereavement.'

'Oh God, I'm sorry. Someone close?'

'Sophie's father.'

'That is bad luck. Please give her my condolences. Been ill long, had he?'

Mark, unwilling to elaborate, shook his head.

'Well, that's a blessing, anyway. Heart attack, I suppose. You're always hearing of them these days. Makes you all the more determined to make hay while the sun shines, doesn't it?'

'Not in the way you mean, no,' Mark said shortly, and Simon gave a light laugh.

'Disapproval duly noted, though if you knew who—'

'I don't want to.'

'So you keep telling me. Well, you'll find out eventually, along with everyone else.'

Mark stopped short, turning to face him. 'You're not still thinking of leaving Jenny?'

'Short of becoming a Mormon, I've no option,' Simon said frivolously.

'You intend to *marry* this woman?'

'That's what I've been telling you for weeks. This one's not just a fling, Mark.'

'Does Jenny know?'

'No, for various reasons we're keeping it under wraps for a while.'

'You don't think you ought to prepare her?'

'No point in worrying her ahead of time.'

Mark started to walk again, shaking his head in disbelief. 'You really are something else, Simon!' he said disgustedly.

At the end of that week, the police having finished their examinations, Lydia moved back to Dormers, and Sophie and Florence went with her. Mark was taken aback; without really considering the matter, he'd assumed that once she left his parents' house they'd all return home. He said as much to Sophie when she informed him of the arrangement.

'Mark, just think about it! Mum hasn't been in the house since the day Daddy died. All his things will be as he left them – clothes in the wardrobe, books on the table, dirty laundry in the basket. You can't expect her to face that alone!'

He moved uncomfortably, resenting being made to feel selfish. 'I assumed Mum would be helping her.'

'We'll *all* help her, but she shouldn't be alone at night just yet. I've promised to stay at least until after the funeral.'

'But God, Sophie,' he protested, 'that could be weeks!'

'So?'

He floundered. 'But what about Florence? What's she supposed to be doing while you settle your mother?'

'Margot offered to have her during the day,' Sophie said coolly – and a shaft of Mark's resentment switched to his mother for not having told him – 'but as you know, the school's roughly halfway between here and home, so she can go back next week.'

'And what exactly is my position in this new arrangement? Am I invited to Dormers too?'

She hesitated. 'If you'd like to come, of course, or you could continue staying here. I'm sure your parents would be glad to have you.'

Unlike you, apparently, he thought silently.

'And if you're worrying about not seeing Florence, of course you could come at weekends.'

He stared at her for a moment, then turned on his heel and left the room.

*   *   *

'Darling, you must make allowances for her,' Margot said gently. 'She's putting her mother first at the moment, and you can't blame her for that.'

'She's shutting me out,' Mark said baldly.

'Of course she isn't, and of course we'd love you to stay on here.'

He sighed and shook his head. 'No, Mum, you need to get back to as near normal as possible, and you have Dad to cope with.'

Although Charles had gone back to work towards the end of that first week, he was still withdrawn and morose and Margot was concerned about him.

'It sounds awful of me,' she confided, 'but I'm hoping he might feel better once Lydia and Sophie have gone. Bless them, they're constant reminders.'

Mark said awkwardly, 'The funeral's supposed to offer "closure", whatever that means. I've always doubted it myself – how can you suddenly start feeling better, when the person who's died remains dead?'

'I think it's when people make an attempt to move on,' Margot said. 'But will you be all right, all by yourself in Chislehurst?'

'Of course I shall. I'll be at work all day, and I can meet Jon sometimes for lunch.'

'And you'll be back at the weekends?'

'Oh yes,' he said a little grimly. 'I'll be back at the weekends.'

Going through her father's things was heartbreaking. Though at first Sophie tried to be composed for her mother's sake it soon proved impossible, and as they opened drawers and leafed through his correspondence they made no attempt to hide their tears. It was both physically and emotionally draining, and after the first couple of days they decided to retire to their rooms for an hour after lunch in order to recoup. Florence meanwhile was back at school, and Margot had offered to collect her each afternoon and take her home for tea, to give them longer to sort things out.

'I shall love having her company,' she'd said.

The question that was haunting them all, Sophie thought as she lay listlessly on her bed one afternoon, was WHY? Why had her father taken his own life without any indication he was considering it, and what had they all done, or not done, to have made him so desperate? Why hadn't he talked to Mum, even to her? What had possessed him to cause them such pain, without so much as an explanation? That ghastly post-mortem had shown him to be a healthy man, so it wasn't some mysterious illness. He and Mum obviously adored each other. And yet, and yet . . . He'd never seemed quite himself since that episode at his birthday party.

She was interrupted in her musings by the chime of her mobile and Stella's name showed on the screen. Oh God, she'd have to tell her what had happened!

'Hi there!' Stella began breezily. 'Just checking on our date this evening. We're meeting the boys at the station as usual, so OK if I call for you at seven thirty?' She waited, and when there was no response added, 'Sophie?'

'Oh Stella,' Sophie began, and the ready tears started again. 'I can't – I'm with Mum. Daddy died the day we came home.'

Stella gasped. 'Oh, you poor lamb! What happened?'

'I – can't go into it now, but as you'll appreciate it's been a total shock for us all.' She started to cry in earnest. 'It's my fault, isn't it? I'm being punished for going with James like that.'

'Now look, honey,' Stella began firmly, 'you can't go thinking like that. Of *course* it's not your fault. Your father must have been ailing for some time, even if you didn't know about it – it was *absolutely* nothing to do with you.' She paused, then asked tentatively, 'How is it with Mark? Is he with you?'

'No. He stayed down all last week while we were at his parents' – or at least, came back each evening – but he's gone home now. He'll come again at the weekend.'

'James is very keen to see you.'

'Too bad, because I don't want to see *him* ever again!'

'Because of your guilt complex about your dad? Get real, Sophie!' Her voice changed. 'Or are you and Mark all lovey-dovey again?'

Sophie sighed. 'No. Actually, it was odd. He was doing his best to comfort me, but I just didn't want him near me.'

'There you are then,' Stella said enigmatically. 'Of course you're upset at the moment – how could you not be? – but it seems obvious to me you still need a bit of spice in your life, and James can supply it.'

'I really can't think about it now, Stella.'

'Fair enough. How long are you staying down there?'

'Till after the funeral, whenever that is.'

'Well I'll give you a bell in a week or two, and we'll see how it goes. In the meantime I really am very sorry about your dad.'

'Thanks,' Sophie said bleakly, and hung up.

The next couple of weeks slowly passed, and since Simon was aware Mark would be returning to an empty house, it proved more difficult to fend off his repeated suggestions of a meal in town. Eventually, since admittedly he was not enjoying his own company at the moment, Mark agreed to accompany him to a gastro pub one evening.

They arrived to find it crowded, and elected to sit at the bar with their drinks until a table became vacant. On the wall in front of them the television droned on inaudibly, lost in the general noise level, while Mark tried to concentrate on Simon's concerns about an upcoming sale. Suddenly he broke off and, glancing at him questioningly, Mark saw his eyes were fixed on the screen. The programme had changed, and Victoria Pyne, a well-known presenter, had appeared on the screen.

'She's married to the boss, isn't she?' he remarked idly. 'Lucky man!'

Simon didn't reply. He'd flushed a deep red and Mark drew in his breath sharply as an alarming suspicion dawned. 'Simon, you're not . . .? I mean, she's not . . .?'

'Got it in one!' Simon said softly. '*Now* do you see what I mean?'

'But – my God! – you're playing with fire on all counts! I mean, she's well known – any hint of scandal and it'll go viral – and the boss, of all people! God, Simon, are you out of your mind?'

'Yes,' Simon said quietly, 'of course I am.'

Mark, lost for words, looked back at the screen. Victoria Pyne, for God's sake! Tall, beautiful, composed, always perfectly groomed – what on earth, he thought uncharitably, did she see in Simon? It couldn't, surely, be serious? Not on her part?

'Are you sure you're not building castles in the air?' he asked. 'She's not likely to want her name spread over the tabloids, is she? And as for your job – well, you can kiss that goodbye.'

'Don't you think she's worth the sacrifice?' Simon said. 'I certainly do.'

A table behind them became vacant and he quickly slipped off his stool to claim it before anyone else could. Mark carried his own glass across. 'Look, you've made this my business by asking me to cover for you. Please, please see sense! It's the cachet of being with a celebrity, isn't it, but Jenny's worth three of her! And think of your children, if your job's expendable. What would this do to them?'

The barman called out a number. Simon said, 'That's our order,' and went to collect it. Setting down the two plates on the table, he added, 'Sorry, Mark, we'll have to agree to disagree on this one. Subject closed.'

In due course the inquest concluded that Peter's death was self-inflicted 'beyond all reasonable doubt' and the date for the funeral was set for Thursday 24 November. Meanwhile Mark continued to go down at weekends and made a point of staying at Dormers, though at times he felt an intruder. Florence at least was delighted to see him, but though he shared Sophie's bed there was no attempt at lovemaking. Was this the end of his marriage? he wondered.

One night, having switched off the bedside light, he said abruptly, 'Who's Lance?' And felt her start violently.

'Lance?' she repeated – to gain time, he thought.

'Yes.' Mark forced himself to speak evenly above the thumping of his heart. 'Apparently he bought Florence an ice cream in Bournemouth, and for some reason you told her not to tell me.'

'Did I?' She sounded flustered. 'I can't think why.'

'Nor can I. So who is he?'

'A friend of Stella's. He happened to be there at the same time, so he looked us up one afternoon.'

'A friend of Stella *and* Rex's, or just of Stella's?'

She moved impatiently. 'She just introduced him as a friend, so how would I know?'

'Oh, you'd know,' he said.

'Why are you making such a thing of this?' she burst out. 'It's not important!'

'It is when our daughter's told to keep something a secret. She was afraid you'd be cross with her if you found out she'd mentioned him.'

'Oh, nonsense! Stop making a mountain out of a molehill and go to sleep!' And she turned on her side to face the wall. 'Goodnight,' she said after a minute.

He did not reply.

Having arranged two days' compassionate leave, Mark took the train home from work on the evening before the funeral, packed himself a weekend case and drove down to Foxbridge, determined that he would return with Sophie and Florence. He was still not happy about the mysterious Lance, and once they were home again and normal life had resumed, he intended to get to the bottom of it. Florence's guilty little face had upset him; she was too young to be taught subterfuge.

He'd been concerned about how his father would stand up to the stresses of the day, but on arrival at his parents' house was surprised to find him in better form than he'd expected, and preparing to deliver the eulogy at the service.

'Are you sure you're up to it, Dad?' he enquired anxiously. 'It'll be very taxing.'

'Of course I'm up to it!' Charles retorted, with a return to his former brusqueness. 'It's the least I can do, as his oldest friend. I owe it to both him and Lydia.'

Mark breathed a sigh of relief, hoping the worst of the shock had worn off and he'd come to terms with what had happened. Now all that remained was to ensure Sophie and Florence's return with him after the funeral.

When they retired to their room that night, he said casually,

'It'll be good to have you both home again. I've been like a lost soul these last weeks.'

She had her back to him, but he sensed her tension. 'Actually, I was going to suggest we stay a bit longer,' she began, her voice falsely casual. 'Planning the funeral has been a terrific strain on Mum – she still needs me.'

'*I* need you, Sophie,' Mark said.

She gave her head an impatient little shake – the only sign she'd heard him. 'In fact, with Christmas only four weeks away, the most sensible thing would be to stay till then.'

She was pretending to fiddle with the zip of her dress, carefully not looking at him. After a minute he said, 'Don't you *want* to come home, Sophie?'

He thought she wasn't going to reply, but then she said in a little voice, 'To be honest, I'm not sure.'

It was as though she'd struck him, yet beneath the immediate shock was the acknowledgement that this was what he'd expected. And beneath *that* lay the so far unadmitted possibility that he mightn't want her to. But he *did* want Florence – quite desperately.

He drew a deep breath, telling himself he must make allowances. Her father's death had hit her hard and she'd always been close to Lydia. He'd no right to force her into important decisions at the moment.

She did turn then, her face pleading with him to understand. 'I'm sorry, Mark, but things haven't been good between us for a while. I think a bit longer apart might be good for both of us.'

'But not for Florence,' he said solidly.

She sighed. 'Yes,' she said, 'she's the one you really miss.'

He started to protest but broke off, not knowing how to defend himself, and it was with an air of armed neutrality that they prepared for bed.

Since the church was less than five minutes' walk from Dormers, the family had elected to follow the hearse on foot and Sophie, who was clutching her mother's arm, seemed grateful for Mark's support. Florence, wide-eyed and wondering, trotted behind them holding the hands of her paternal grand-parents, with Jonathan and Delia bringing up the rear.

After Jon's account of her reaction to Peter's death, Mark had studied Delia more closely than usual, but although she appeared tense there was, thank goodness, no indication of another outburst.

It was a bright winter's day, with frost in sheltered places where the sun hadn't reached and a clear blue sky, and there was an eerie quietness as they walked, the song of a bird the only other sound. Then, with shocking suddenness, the church bell began to toll. Mark felt a lump come into his throat and Sophie's fingers momentarily tightened on his.

As they rounded the corner they could see a long line of cars clogging the narrow lane and there was barely room for the hearse to pass. Then they were turning into the church gateway and the minister was at the door waiting to receive them. The coffin was removed from the hearse, bearing a single wreath of red roses, and they processed inside while the minister proclaimed, 'I am the resurrection and the life, saith the Lord . . .' As they were shown into the reserved pews, Mark noted that both Sophie and Lydia were pale but composed, and was proud of them.

As had been apparent from the cars outside, there was a large congregation and the little country church was packed. Peter Kingsley had been well known and well-liked and his death had shocked many people. Apart from the village, which appeared to have turned out in force, Mark later learned there were representatives from Rotary, from the golf club and from the firm for which Peter and Charles worked, as well as a fairly large contingent of Kingsley relatives, most of whom he didn't recall having seen before.

The service followed its time-honoured ritual and Mark, who had tensed when his father rose to give the eulogy, began to relax as Charles spoke strongly and movingly about his long friendship with Peter, interspersing amusing anecdotes of misadventures they'd shared over the years. When he returned to his pew Lydia gratefully squeezed his hand.

The final hymn 'Guide Me, O Thou Great Redeemer', a favourite of Peter's since his rugby-playing days, brought the indoor proceedings to an end and the congregation moved outside to the prepared graveside. Most of the funerals Mark had attended involved cremations, and it was some time since he'd attended an interment. Standing among the gravestones and reading their heartfelt inscriptions added to his sadness, and he was glad when it was time to return to Dormers.

The warmth of the house was welcome after the chilly graveyard, and those who had elected to attend the wake began to relax, helping themselves to the tempting array of food laid out by the caterers and, now that the serious part of the day was behind them, exchanging happier memories of Peter. Several of them were meeting for the first time in years, and were catching up on family news. Mark spoke to two couples who'd attended Peter and Lydia's wedding and another who, along with his own mother and father, were Sophie's godparents. It was some time before he realized he'd not seen his father for a while and, his heart sinking, went in search of him.

He found Charles in Peter's study, sitting in the chair behind his desk, a glass of whisky in his hand.

'OK, Dad?'

Charles looked up and gave a brief nod.

'The eulogy was just right – well done.' He paused, and when his father made no comment said tentatively, 'Are you coming back to the sitting room? People will want to speak to you.'

'They're Peter's friends, not mine,' Charles said expressionlessly, 'and they'd want nothing to do with me if they knew I'd killed him.'

'Dad!' Mark stared at him in shock. 'What are you talking about? Of course you—'

'I killed him,' Charles continued over him, 'as surely as if I'd strung him up on that shower rail.'

'How can you possibly think that?' Mark protested vehemently. 'You were his oldest friend!'

Charles gave a harsh laugh. 'What I did was hardly indicative of friendship.'

Though he'd much rather not have known, Mark felt compelled to press him further. 'So what was that?' he challenged.

'You'll despise me when I tell you. I despise myself.'

'Try me.'

'Confession time? Very well.' He drew a deep breath. 'To my everlasting shame, I sent him an anonymous letter.' He paused, holding Mark's gaze. 'The week before his sixtieth birthday.'

ELEVEN

Clapham, London; November

'It's just so *unfair*!' Ellie said vehemently, pushing her untouched plate away from her. 'One mistake when she was my age, and she paid for it the rest of her life!'

Tom smiled. 'I'm quite sure she didn't consider you a mistake!'

She brushed away his attempt at humour. 'It was what she went through when I was born that made her a semi-invalid. She nearly *died*, Tom!'

He took a long slow drink of beer. 'She never gave any hint who your father was?'

Ellie shook her head. 'She always insisted it was a one-night stand and she was drunk, and I more or less accepted that. But something Gran said the other day made me wonder.'

'What was that?'

'Well, I was on about what a rotten life Mum had had, and she muttered something about that's what happened when you got involved with a married man. Then she looked shocked, as though she'd not meant to say it aloud, and I couldn't get anything else out of her.'

'So the odds are she knows who he was.'

'That's what I thought, and surely I of all people have a right to know!' She brightened. 'I suppose I could try to trace him. People do trace their birth parents, don't they?'

'I think that's when you've been adopted.'

'But there must still be ways. And if it *was* a married man, he ought at least to have made provision for her – us – accepted some responsibility.'

'If he was drunk too he mightn't even have known who she was.'

Ellie shook her head. 'I never really believed the drunk bit. Gran has often said what a shy girl Mum was, which

doesn't sound like the type to go out and get drunk, then
sleep with a stranger. Or anyone, come to that.' She paused,
then added wistfully, 'I'd much rather it had been someone
she loved.'

'Well,' Tom said philosophically, 'we'll never know, will
we?'

She gazed reflectively into her wine glass. 'I wish she could
at least have been here for Christmas. She always loved it,
insisted on having a real tree and everything. It'll be horrible
without her.' Her eyes filled and Tom put a hand over hers.
'*Why* do people have to die near to Christmas? It makes it so
much worse, somehow. It was the same with Gramps, two
years ago. Now there's only me and Gran.'

Which meant, Tom thought disconsolately, there was even
less chance of Ellie moving in with him. He'd known her just
over a year and inevitably had also come to know her family.
Sybil Mallory, the grandmother, had on first acquaintance
struck him as a capable, no-nonsense type of woman, but her
attitude towards both her daughter and granddaughter betrayed
deep affection for them.

Fay, Ellie's mother, had been harder to assess; he'd only
ever seen her on the couch in the living room, often with a
rug over her knees. Pale and thin, there had still been a trace
of blonde prettiness about her and it was perhaps unworthy
of him to suspect that she tended to play on her weakness.
There was no denying she'd had a raw deal; according to Ellie,
as a young girl she'd been keen on tennis and dancing, activities that, along with much else, had been denied her from the
age of twenty following what had reportedly been a difficult
pregnancy and a long-drawn-out birth. At twenty-two himself,
the thought of such restriction appalled him.

And then there was the mysterious lover . . .

'I'd better be getting back.' Ellie's voice broke into his
reflections. 'Gran wants us to start going through Mum's
things.'

'God, it's a bit soon, isn't it?'

'She says it'll get harder the longer we leave it. To tell you
the truth, I'm dreading it.'

It was a Saturday afternoon and he'd assumed they would

spend it together. However, Ellie's dead mother had priority. 'How about the cinema later?' he suggested without much hope, and she shook her head.

'Perhaps next week.'

He walked her back through the dank November streets to her gate and they kissed goodbye. She had started up the path when she turned and looked back at him. 'Tom, if I *do* try to trace my father, will you help me?'

He made a movement of protest. 'Oh, now look, El . . .'

'Please?'

Reluctantly he nodded. It would probably come to nothing anyway. 'OK,' he said.

It was a gruelling few days. While carols blared remorselessly from radios and shopping centres, Sybil and Ellie, often fighting tears, went through Fay's clothes and personal possessions, dividing them into piles for keeping, for taking to charity shops and for recycling. Not, Ellie thought sadly, that she'd had a great deal. Her trinket box contained only costume jewellery in outdated settings and, though she couldn't bear to part with it, she knew she'd never wear it. There were one or two cashmere sweaters that her grandmother thought she should keep, but the memory of her mother in them was too recent, and she put them on the charity pile.

'What are we going to do about Christmas?' she asked at one point.

Her grandmother tipped the contents of Fay's makeup drawer into the bin. 'What do you want to do?'

'Ignore it,' Ellie said promptly.

'Then that's what we'll do. We'll forget the turkey; I'll get a nice leg of lamb, and you can watch some of your boxed sets instead of the television. I must warn you, though, we'll still get cards, even if we don't send them.'

'Perhaps we should send just a few, to tell people about Mum?'

'I've had some printed for that,' Sybil said.

They hadn't a car, and it was necessary to make several trips to the charity shop, where their offerings were received with delight. After depositing the last load they returned home with the forlorn satisfaction of a job well done.

Sybil immediately made her way to the kitchen to prepare lunch, but Ellie went up to the denuded room and stood dejectedly looking about her. It no longer seemed like her mother's; the bed linen had been removed and a cotton spread covered the mattress, while the dressing table looked heartbreakingly bare, cleared of Fay's bottles and jars. She sat down on the stool, glanced at her pale face in the mirror and mindlessly opened one drawer after another to stare down into its empty cavity. The bottom one on the right needed an extra push to shut it, and even then didn't close flush with the rest.

Frowning, she jiggled it about, but as there still seemed to be an obstruction she lifted it out and, feeling around at the back of the gap, her fingers closed on a thin piece of card. Drawing it out, she found herself looking at a crumpled postcard with a view of a promenade and a stretch of golden sand. Underneath it were printed the words *Drumlee, Angus.*

On the flip side was a brief message, headed *The Merlin Hotel, 6 July 1999* which read: *Sorry to hear you won't be up this summer. Perhaps this card will change your mind?! Best – Lexie and Callum.*

But it was the name and address alongside that accelerated her heartbeat. It had originally been sent to Mr and Mrs Douglas Crawford, The Beeches, Pendleton Drive, Knutsford, Cheshire. However, the words 'and Mrs' had been crossed out in biro and a London address substituted for the Cheshire one. Above it, in a more childish hand, were scrawled the words *Please, Dad! H* and three kisses.

Ellie sat motionless, excitement building inside her. She had the feeling that what she held was momentous, if she could only decipher it. What did it mean, and how in the name of goodness did it come to be at the back of her mother's drawer? 1999 – the year before she was born. Her heart set up a heavy, uneven beat. *Douglas Crawford*: was it remotely possible that he could be her father?

'Ellie?'

She jumped as her grandmother's voice reached her.

'Lunch is ready.'

'Coming,' she called back. Then, without analysing her action, she ran across the landing to her own room and, opening a drawer at random, slipped the card under a pile of handkerchiefs, resolving to say nothing until she'd had time to consider her find.

The next day Sybil went down with a dose of flu – an emotional reaction, the doctor suggested, to the trauma of the last few weeks. The final clearance of her daughter's room must have sapped the last of her strength.

Fortunately Ellie was able to look after her, the secretarial college she was attending having granted her compassionate leave until the end of term. Though she'd no particular desire to learn word-processing, text production or business communications, both Sybil and Fay had decreed it would stand her in good stead while she decided what she wanted to do with her life. All it had achieved thus far, however, was to convince her she did not want to be a legal secretary.

The daily tasks of attending to her grandmother, collecting her prescriptions, doing the shopping and cooking tempting meals meant she'd not yet had a chance to share her secret with Tom, and it was not until the following weekend, when he rang asking after Sybil and hoping Ellie might be free, that she was able to arrange to meet him. In the meantime, she had repeatedly taken out the hidden postcard, poring over it in the vain hope that it might resolve some of her unanswered questions.

Tom looked up from the postcard, meeting her expectant gaze.

'Oh, cripes!' he said.

'It could be him, couldn't it, Tom? The dates fit.'

'They could fit all kinds of things. Look, El, you've not a shred of proof this man has anything to do with you.'

'Then why did Mum keep his postcard for nearly twenty years?'

'It was stuck at the back of a drawer. She'd have forgotten all about it.'

'But she must have put it there in the first place. Come on, Tom, admit it! It *could* be him, couldn't it?'

'So could the man in the moon.'

'Now you're just being silly!' she said crossly.

'All right, but I don't see what you can do about it.'

'I could contact him,' she said.

His eyes widened in dismay. 'God, no, Ellie, you can't!'

'*Why* can't I?'

'Think about it! He's obviously a married man, and that "Dad" means he has kids as well. You can't just drop a bomb-shell into their midst after nearly twenty years!'

She leaned towards him. 'Tom, that man – if he *is* my father – is responsible for the miserable life Mum led! If it hadn't been for him, she'd have been happy and healthy and able to lead a normal life.'

'You don't know that,' Tom argued. 'It might have been something to do with her insides that would have caused problems whoever she was or wasn't married to.'

'It might have been his genes,' Ellie said, but she no longer sounded so confident.

Tom shook his head. 'My advice is to forget it. Throw the card away. No good will come of it.'

She snatched it back from him. 'Certainly not!' She glanced down at it. 'I looked up Drumlee on my old school atlas. It's quite a long way up. I could at least find out if this hotel's still going. It says sorry they're not going up *that year*, so it sounds as though these people often met them there, in which case the owners might remember them.'

'It might have changed hands,' Tom said flatly.

'Look it up on your phone!' she said, excitement ringing in her voice. 'You can get the internet, can't you?'

He moved uncomfortably. 'Look, Ellie, I really think you should forget this.'

'Go on! What harm can it do? The Merlin Hotel, Drumlee.'

Reluctantly he typed it in and a moment later text appeared on the screen.

'What does it say?' Ellie asked eagerly.

'*Situated in the centre of the bustling town of Drumlee yet only five minutes from the beach, the Merlin Hotel is a family-owned hotel offering comfortable accommodation and first-class home cooking. Wide-screen television and WiFi in*

all rooms. Ample parking. Conference facilities. Private func-
tions catered for. Championship golf course within easy reach.
An excellent centre for walking and boating holidays.'

He passed her the phone. 'There's a photo and a map.'

Ellie studied the long, low building with interest. It had
been photographed across a square, the centre of which was
taken up with a colourful display of flowerbeds.

'I wonder if he still goes there,' she mused. 'In which case,
if it's a family-run hotel, the owners probably *do* know him.'

'They might know Douglas Crawford,' Tom said deliberately, 'but that certainly doesn't mean they know your dad.'

At supper that evening, Ellie took her courage in both hands.
'Gran, is there really nothing you can tell me about my father?'

Sybil, still pale from her illness, drew in her lips. 'Ellie,
how many times—'

'But you said something once about a married man,' Ellie
burst out, unable to keep quiet any longer.

Sybil drew in her breath. 'I don't know what you're talking
about,' she blustered.

'Something about Mum bringing it on herself by going with
a married man?'

Her grandmother closed her eyes. 'God help me if I said
that. I certainly didn't mean it.'

'But *was* he married, my dad? If you know that much, you
must know who he is!'

There was a long silence. Sybil's bony fingers were pleating
the napkin in her lap. At last she gave a deep sigh. 'All right,
love, I'll tell you all I know, but it's very little. She began to
get friendly with a man at the office – older than she was. She
never told us his name, only that he lived up north somewhere
and was here on a year's sabbatical. We didn't like the sound
of it, especially when she finally admitted he was married.'

She shook her head sadly. 'Fay had always been such a
biddable girl, never giving us any trouble. But these quiet ones
can be stubborn, and nothing we said made any difference.'
She met Ellie's sympathetic eyes. 'The trouble was she was
head-over-heels, poor lamb.'

'So she *did* love him!' Ellie exclaimed.

'Oh, there was never any doubt of that. Whether *he* loved *her*, or was just amusing himself while away from home, is another matter. One thing I will say in his defence, though: he didn't know she was pregnant, because nor did she until he'd gone back home, and she refused point-blank to contact him. "I went into it with my eyes open," she said, "and I'm *glad* I'm having his baby!"'

Ellie's eyes filled. 'So I *was* wanted!' she whispered.

Sybil reached for her hand. 'You were *always* wanted, my darling. You lit up our lives from the word go.'

Ellie drew a quavering breath. So at last she had *some* answers. Perhaps they would be enough.

TWELVE

Kent

Mark stared at his father in stupefied disbelief. 'You did *what*?'

Charles drained the remaining whisky in his glass. 'I think you heard,' he said.

'But – I don't understand! Why on earth – and what—' He broke off in confusion.

'As to *why*, because I was in a state of shock and reacted on the spur of the moment. Believe me, if I could have snatched that letter back, I would have.' He twirled the empty glass in his fingers, looking down on it. 'As to what I reacted *to*, that's a different matter.'

Mark moistened his lips. 'But – was it something to do with work?'

Charles smiled thinly. 'You mean had he been misappropriating funds? No, nothing so simple.'

'But surely not an affair? He and Aunt Lydia—'

'Adored each other,' his father finished for him. 'That was certainly the received wisdom. Yet it *was* an affair – of a sort.' He looked up, meeting his son's eyes. 'The homosexual sort,' he ended deliberately.

Mark reached for the chair behind him and lowered himself into it. After a minute he said flatly, 'I don't believe it!'

'I'd have had difficulty believing it myself if I'd not seen them together. And though what I did was unforgivable, it was chiefly on Lydia's behalf.' Lydia, whom, though his son didn't know it, he'd loved for most of his life. 'How in God's name could he do that to her?'

The last sentence was spoken so softly Mark had difficulty hearing it. He moistened his lips again. 'But couldn't you have been mistaken? I mean, it might just have been . . .' His voice petered helplessly out.

'No mistake. It was last August; Peter and I had attended a board meeting that overran, and since it was getting late several of us decided to have a meal before going home, and rang to let our wives know. Then, when we reached the restaurant, Peter announced that as he had a headache coming on he'd cry off and go home after all.

'Naturally I never gave it another thought. Until, that is, a couple of hours later, when I was in a cab on my way to the station. We'd pulled up at a red light and suddenly there he was, as large as life, coming out of a hotel in Buckingham Palace Road, his hand on the shoulder of a young man. Even then, though puzzled, I might have dismissed it, but at that moment a taxi drew up. He bent to speak to the driver, before opening the door for the boy, who' – Charles broke off and passed a hand over his face – 'gave him a quick kiss before getting in. Then the lights changed and my own cab moved on.'

There was a long silence while Mark tried frantically to think of something to say. Eventually he stammered, 'Could it have been some relation – a nephew or someone, who—'

'Who would never have kissed him on the lips.' Charles gave a deep sigh. 'No, he was no relation of Peter's, but he could almost be regarded as one of ours.'

Mark stared at him blankly.

'It was the Firth boy,' Charles said heavily. 'Delia's gay brother.'

The rest of the wake passed in a blur for Mark. Sick and disorientated, he was unsure whether Peter's actions or his father's response to them had caused the greater shock. Not to mention the link with Delia which, involving the family as it did, added to the complications. At least this explained to some degree her reaction to his death. Odd, he reflected, that while he was open-minded about the sexual proclivities of her brother or indeed any other gay men, Peter Kingsley was a different matter entirely.

Yet surely there was an inconsistency here: if Peter had received Charles's letter just before his birthday, it would certainly account for his behaviour at the party. But he must have weathered it to some degree, since it was another three months before he took his own life. What had finally tipped him over the edge?

His eyes moved over the subdued throng, soberly dressed as befitted the occasion, and came to rest on Sophie and his mother chatting to Lydia. Did they deserve to know the cause of Peter's suicide which, unresolved, would haunt them for the rest of their lives? Or was it better that they remain in ignorance? For any hint of the truth would raise a permanent and impenetrable barrier between the two families.

'You look in need of another drink, bro!' said a voice beside him, and he turned to see Jonathan holding out a glass. He nodded, took it and drank from it. Jonathan frowned.

'You OK?'

Mark cleared his throat. 'Not really. Jon, we need to talk. Soon.'

'Sure, but is something wrong?'

'I'm afraid so, but now's not the time to go into it.'

'Lunch on Monday, then? The usual place?'

Mark shook his head. 'I think Delia should be there.'

'Hey, what is this? You're beginning to worry me.'

From the corner of his eye, Mark saw his father appear in the doorway, to be immediately incorporated into the nearest group. He prayed fervently that he'd say nothing to alert suspicion.

Since he hadn't replied, Jonathan added, 'Do you want us to meet after work, then? I'd suggest you came back for a meal, but no doubt you'll be wanting to get home to the family.'

Mark said aridly, 'Sophie intends to stay here till Christmas.'

After a beat of silence Jonathan laid a hand on his arm. 'I'm sorry,' he said quietly. 'Well, if you'd be going back to an empty house, come for a meal and stay the night. We can go in to work together the next morning.'

'That's good of you, Jon.'

'Text me when you're leaving the office and we can travel back together.'

Feeling marginally more cheerful, Mark moved on to mingle with the assorted guests.

As the atmosphere between himself and Sophie was still fraught, it seemed wise not to prolong his visit and, resisting pressure from his mother to stay for the weekend – which would also entail the enforced company of his father – it was with a sense of relief that Mark made his excuses and set off for home that same evening. It had been a traumatic visit in more ways than one – the funeral itself, his father's confession and Sophie's bombshell. The empty house in Chislehurst would seem like a refuge, but a brief one since soon he'd have to face Delia. Did she know something they didn't about Peter's death?

He slept badly that weekend, the nights peppered with dreams that dissolved before he could dissect them but left a feeling of unease, and when he reached the office on Monday he felt decidedly underslept. It did not help that Simon was more importunate than ever, adding to his stress levels.

'When can we speak?' he persisted, breaching Mark's avoidance strategy. 'I need you to cover for me.'

'For God's sake, Simon,' Mark snapped, 'why don't you sort yourself out?' Then, seeing the other man's face, added, 'Look, I'm sorry, but I've had a lousy weekend and now I'm snowed under with work.'

'Lunch?' Simon enquired hopefully.

'It'll be a sandwich at my desk.'

'A drink after work, then?'

'Sorry, I'm meeting my brother.'

Simon shrugged disconsolately and, accepting temporary defeat, at last moved away.

Mark had decided not to mention the anonymous letter. He'd have had no hesitation in revealing the full facts to Jonathan, but he was even less sure of Delia than he'd been before and didn't want to expose Charles's failings to a possibly hostile audience.

As arranged, the brothers met at Waterloo and journeyed out to Barnes together.

'Sorry to hear Sophie's staying down there,' Jonathan said. 'It must be rotten being on your own for so long.'

'To tell you the truth, Jon, I don't think she's ever coming back.'

Jonathan's head swung towards him. 'God, Mark! Why? What's happened?'

'Nothing dramatic, we've just drifted apart. It's obvious she no longer wants to spend time with me, and to be honest the feeling's mutual.'

Jonathan looked at him shrewdly. 'Anyone else involved?'

'In my case, no. In hers, I'm not so sure. She spent a week in Bournemouth with Stella and the kids over half-term, and Florence spoke of an "Uncle Lance" whom they'd met down there. Then she flushed and said Sophie told her not to mention him.' He shrugged. 'It might be nothing, but Peter's death coming immediately after they got back meant I've not been able to question her fully.'

After a brief silence Jonathan said, 'I might be speaking out of turn, but I've always felt you were at a disadvantage when it came to Soph and her father. He never denied her anything, did he? I can remember occasions when you refused to go ahead with some extravagant purchase and she promptly went to him and was given it.'

Mark smiled ruefully. 'It was difficult, yes. Made me look either stingy or a pauper – or both!'

Jonathan laughed. 'Well, I hope things work out, one way or another.'

They were drawing into their station, and to Mark's relief the subject was dropped.

As Delia worked locally in a public relations agency she was home before them, and an appetizing aroma met the two men as they came into the house. She emerged from the kitchen to greet them, still dressed in the formal clothes she wore to work and with no concession to culinary duties, and presented a cool cheek to her husband and brother-in-law in turn for a perfunctory kiss.

'So, Mark, we meet again,' she commented. 'The spare room's ready for you, if you'd care to take your case up.'

'I'll show you where it is,' Jonathan offered. 'You might like to freshen up before we eat.'

Mark had, in fact, been to their home only once before, to a formal dinner with Sophie and his parents soon after the wedding. Tucked away at the end of a quiet cul-de-sac, it was what estate agents liked to refer to as a 'bijou residence' – in other words a small but elegant-looking house, well-proportioned and with expensive fittings. There were only two bedrooms, but both were en suite and tastefully decorated and Mark looked about him admiringly. He'd noted that Delia used the term 'spare' bedroom rather than 'guest' – possibly, he thought, amused, because they hadn't intended to have overnight visitors.

'Come down when you're ready and we'll have a drink,' Jonathan said.

Left to himself, Mark unpacked his meagre belongings, laying his night clothes on one of the twin beds and taking his sponge bag through to the bathroom. He was not looking forward to the next hour or so.

Downstairs there was only one entertaining room but it was of a good size, and the small rosewood dining table with matching chairs took up barely a quarter of it. Jonathan and Delia were waiting for him.

'I believe you've something important to tell us,' Delia said without preamble as Jonathan handed Mark his usual whisky and soda. 'I wasn't sure if you were intending this to take place before or after the meal, so it's a casserole that will come to no harm if kept waiting.'

'But I hope it's before,' Jonathan cut in with an anxious smile, 'because I'm consumed with curiosity. In the meantime, cheers!'

They all lifted their glasses and drank, Mark grateful for the comforting warmth as it went down his throat. In the Richmond family whisky was never served with ice. 'If you'd like me to get straight down to it, fair enough,' he said. In truth he'd be glad to get the ordeal over.

Delia motioned him to an easy chair beside the fake log fire and seated herself on the sofa. After a momentary hesitation, Jonathan took his place beside her.

Mark stared down into his glass, trying to find the most palatable phrases. 'I asked for Delia to be present because she's the one most concerned in this,' he began. He looked up, meeting her suddenly wary eyes. 'It's to do with your brother,' he said.

She gave a little gasp as Jonathan exclaimed, 'Robin? How on earth?'

Mark bit his lip, addressing himself to her. 'I think you know, don't you? That he was . . . involved . . . with Peter Kingsley?'

'*Involved?*' Jonathan repeated incredulously. 'What the hell do you mean, involved?'

'Sexually,' Mark said. When he dared look at Delia, he saw the colour had drained from her face.

'Good God, Mark, what are you *talking* about? *Peter?*' And when he didn't reply Jonathan turned to his wife, noticing her distress for the first time. 'Darling?' he queried uncertainly. Then, 'This can't be right, surely?'

Ignoring him, she looked straight at Mark. 'How much do you know?'

'Only what I've told you,' he replied.

'But *how* do you know?' Jonathan burst out. 'If there's anything in it, that is, which I don't believe for a minute!'

'They were seen together,' Mark said steadily.

'By whom?'

He shook his head.

'But that's nonsense!' Jonathan insisted. 'They didn't even know each other, and Peter . . . well, Peter—'

Delia laid a cold hand over his. 'Hush,' she said. 'If he knows that much he might as well hear all of it.'

Jonathan turned to her in bewilderment. 'What do you mean, all of it?'

'That I killed Peter Kingsley.'

The two men stared at her, stunned into silence. This, Mark thought almost hysterically, was the second confession to murder he'd heard in a few days. Since Jonathan seemed incapable of speech, he cleared his throat. 'I think you'd better explain.'

'They met at our wedding,' she said, speaking slowly and without emphasis, 'and there was an immediate attraction – that's what Robin told me. Of course no one noticed, all eyes were on us, the *bridal pair*.' A note of irony. 'But Peter managed to slip Rob a note, asking him to meet for a drink the next week. Rob could hardly believe it, this handsome, popular family man being interested in him, especially when there was such a huge age gap. He'd only ever been with people his own age.'

She looked down at her tightly clasped hands. Neither man prompted her and after a pause she went on. 'So they met, but Rob saw at once that Peter wasn't comfortable. He blurted out that this had never happened to him before, that he was in love with his wife – all the usual platitudes. Nevertheless, they met twice more in different hotels and by then Rob was deeply in love.'

She looked up and now her eyes were full of tears. 'Then, in the middle of August Peter phoned in a panic and said someone had seen them. He was all for calling it off then and there, but Rob managed to talk him out of it.' She paused again. 'Naturally, I didn't know any of this at the time; it was only when I happened to mention how oddly Peter behaved at his birthday party that it all came out. I was appalled, convinced it could only end in disaster.'

She sighed. 'But Robin wouldn't listen and the relationship limped on, though Peter was continually on edge, saying he shouldn't be there and worried someone else would see them. Again, I wasn't aware of this because, knowing my opinion, Rob was avoiding me and I didn't actually see him for some time. But I became increasingly concerned about him, kept texting and leaving phone messages though he never got back to me. I even went round to his flat once, but he wasn't there.'

'Why didn't you *tell* me?' Jonathan asked in a low voice. 'You shouldn't have gone through all that alone.'

Delia lifted her shoulders. 'How could I? Look how you reacted just now. You hero-worshipped Peter – you'd known him all your life. You'd have put all the blame on Robin.'

'But I still don't understand how you can feel responsible for his death. That's just—'

She lifted a hand and he subsided. 'It was several weeks before I tracked Rob down, and I was shocked at the change in him. He'd lost weight and looked ghastly, and I finally got out of him what had happened. A few weeks previously they'd met at some out-of-the-way pub, and without warning Peter just blurted out that it was over – that he couldn't go on any longer. It had been a "temporary madness", he said, and he was deeply sorry to have involved Rob in what he referred to as "this gross foolishness".

'Rob, needless to say, was distraught and broke down while he was telling me. Well, as you can imagine I was absolutely blazing; this much older man had seduced my brother, then suddenly, with no consideration of his feelings, brought every-thing to an abrupt end, and I didn't see why he should get away with it.'

She drew a deep breath. 'So instead of being sensible and waiting till my fury had simmered down, I promptly rang Peter at his office and accused him of seduction and playing fast and loose with my brother's feelings. I asked him if he'd any idea what damage he'd done to Rob, and what he thought his wife would say if she knew about it. And then I slammed down the phone. Of course I'd no intention of telling Lydia – I just wanted to bring home to him what he'd done.'

'Two days later,' she ended expressionlessly, 'I heard that he'd hanged himself.'

She covered her face with her hands and the mantelpiece clock ticked into the prolonged silence. Jonathan put an arm round her and drew her against him, his face now as strained as hers, and Mark cursed himself for coming here in the first place. Why hadn't he just let things unravel – or not – in their own time?

'One minute, though,' Jonathan said suddenly. 'How did Peter *know* someone had seen them?'

Mark shook his head.

'Then how did *you* know?'

'Leave it, Jon.'

'No, dammit, I won't leave it! This other person, whoever he or she was, is the one who precipitated it, possibly by threatening to expose him. It wasn't only down to Delia.'

Delia had removed her hands and was staring at Mark, a glimmer of hope in her eyes. So in the end he'd no choice after all.

'I was hoping not to have to tell you this,' he said, 'but you're right; it wasn't only Delia. Dad cast the first stone.'

'*Dad?*'

Mark felt a spurt of sympathy for his brother, having to accept that not only his wife but his father had had a hand in the tragedy. 'He told me after the funeral. I was still in shock when you came up and handed me that drink.'

'So he'd already had it out with Peter?'

'No,' Mark said heavily. 'To his everlasting shame he sent an anonymous letter.'

The look of horror on Jonathan's face mirrored his own reaction.

'I don't believe it!' he said, for the second time that evening. But Mark knew that he did. He turned to Delia. 'Does Robin know what's happened?'

She nodded.

'How is he?'

'How do you think?'

'Will he be all right?'

She nodded again. 'He's stronger than he thinks.'

Jonathan stood up suddenly. 'I'm going to refresh our drinks. God knows we need it.'

Mark said awkwardly, 'I'm so sorry, Delia.'

She shook her head tiredly. 'It's better that it should all come out. Secrets are corrosive.'

Jonathan handed them their refilled glasses. 'There's another thing,' he said, sitting down with his own drink. 'What you've told us has been of some comfort to Dee, but Dad must also have been going through hell; he shouldn't have to go on bearing the entire blame, either.'

They both looked anxiously at Delia, and she slowly nodded. 'That's only fair,' she acknowledged. 'It must have hit him hard; they've been lifelong friends, haven't they?'

'More or less,' Mark confirmed. 'What concerns me, though, is whether we should tell the others – Mum, Lydia and Sophie.'

'No!' Jonathan said sharply. 'What possible good would that do?'

'Stop them torturing themselves, wondering why he did it.'

'It might be worse if they knew. Lydia might even wonder if her whole marriage had been a sham.'

'Then let's leave it to Dad to decide,' Mark said, and there the matter rested.

*   *   *

God, what a mess it all was! he thought as he left Jonathan at Waterloo the next morning. Apart from the dread of speaking to his father – which they'd decided they would do together at the weekend – there was his relationship with Sophie to sort out. And as if all that wasn't enough, Simon was sailing close to the wind. If his affair with Victoria Pyne came out, in all likelihood he'd take Mark, his unwilling alibi, down with him. It was not a promising prospect.

Delia refused to go down with them. 'It'll be easier without me there,' she insisted. 'I'll arrange a weekend visit to my chief bridesmaid; she's always asking me over.'

Margot was delighted at the prospect of having her sons to stay. 'You won't be at Dormers, then?' she asked, when Mark rang to tell her.

'I'll probably spend Sunday there,' he replied.

'You must make allowances for Sophie, darling; she's—'

'I'm always making allowances for her,' he interrupted, and she wisely didn't persist.

It had been arranged that Jonathan should accompany Mark back to Chislehurst on the Friday evening and they'd drive down together the following day. It was the first weekend in December, and every window seemed to be sporting a Christmas tree.

'I haven't bought a single present,' Mark said gloomily. 'Sophie and I have always gone shopping together.'

'Why don't you suggest it when you see her? It might be a means of getting back together, even if only temporarily.'

Mark simply shrugged. 'You'll be well out of the family gathering, down in Devon,' he said. 'For two pins, I'd come with you!'

'I doubt if it'll be a bundle of laughs there, either, with Robin in his present state.'

'He'll no doubt put on a brave face in front of his parents.'

'Families!' Jonathan commented, and they both laughed.

Both the brothers had been apprehensive about meeting their father, but though he cast a wary glance at Mark he seemed much the same as always. They'd been wondering how to spirit him away from Margot, but over coffee on their arrival she solved the problem for them.

'I promised to do the church flowers this weekend before I knew you were coming,' she said. 'So I suggest you three men take yourselves off for a pub lunch and perhaps a good long walk, since you two have been cooped up in London. Then we can meet again for tea. I made one of my Dundee cakes, which I know you can't resist!'

'An excellent idea!' Jonathan said heartily. 'Do we build up an appetite by having our walk first, or work off our lunch with exercise after?'

'Walk first, while the weather holds,' Charles decreed. 'Rain's forecast for later.'

They set off along the country lanes and turned into a copse that had been a favourite haunt when the boys were young. The summer's foliage, depressingly brown and soggy, lay underfoot and through the bare branches an increasingly dark sky was visible.

For a while they walked in silence. Then Charles said abruptly, 'Well, we might as well get it over with. No doubt you've both come down to chastise me, so feel free. You can't call me anything I've not called myself.'

'Actually, Dad, we hope what we have to say might help a little.'

Charles looked at them sharply. 'Go on.'

Jonathan steeled himself. 'Robin told Delia about the . . . affair,' he began. 'And no, before you ask, she didn't say anything to me. Not then.'

'And how does that mitigate my actions?'

Jonathan continued as if he hadn't spoken. 'As you'd expect, she was very upset, knowing it could only end in disaster.' He paused. 'Peter panicked when he received your letter and wanted to end it, but Robin pleaded with him and it continued for another month or so. Then Peter just broke it off – somewhat brutally, it has to be said. Robin was devastated and took pains to avoid Delia, knowing she'd not approved in the first place. But she finally tracked him down, and was shocked at the state he was in. He told her what had happened and she blew her top.'

Jonathan drove his hands further into the pockets of his greatcoat, his eyes on the ground. 'So she rang Peter at the office, gave him hell, and asked him how he thought Lydia would feel if she found out.'

Charles made an exclamation under his breath.

'And two days later,' Jonathan continued stoically, 'well . . . you know what happened.'

Instinctively they'd all stopped walking and stood in a small knot under the naked trees. Jonathan forced himself to go on.

'Obviously she'd no intention of telling Lydia, she just wanted him to know the hurt he'd caused her brother. But we all felt you should know you weren't wholly to blame.'

There was a long silence. Then Charles laid a hand on his son's shoulder. 'Thanks, Jon; that can't have been easy, and I'm grateful to both you and Delia for telling me. It doesn't make what I did any more forgivable, but at least it wasn't the final straw. And from her angle, it wouldn't have got to that stage without my letter, so she can take some comfort from that.'

'That's generous of you, Dad,' Jonathan murmured. Mark suspected that he was close to tears, and cleared his throat.

'After all of which, I think it's time we turned our feet pubwards and downed a couple of pints of good strong ale.'

The other two smiled. 'I'll second that,' Charles said and, with a feeling of relief, they turned their steps in the direction of the Plough.

The following day, Sophie told Mark that she'd decided not to return to Chislehurst in the near future. 'I think we'd both benefit from a longer time apart,' she said.

'Lance?' Mark asked bitterly, before he could stop himself. Somehow, though he'd been expecting this and had told his brother the feeling was mutual, he felt unaccountably hurt.

She looked at him quickly. 'I told you, he's Stella's friend, not mine. Honestly, Mark. That's the truth.'

And he had to believe her. Not, he concluded, that it was much consolation.

THIRTEEN

Kent

I t had been a miserable Christmas. Lydia, Sophie and
Florence had moved into the Richmond home for the holiday,
but no amount of tinsel could disguise the underlying
tension, and only Florence remained unaware of it. Peter's
absence was a constant sadness and though Mark and Sophie
valiantly strove to appear at ease with each other, no one
except their little daughter was fooled.

The number of guests had made it necessary for them to
share their usual bedroom. No one alluded to the fact; Sophie
had tightened her lips but made no comment, and Mark
wondered miserably if all three parents hoped some miracle
might bring them back together. If so, they were doomed to
disappointment.

And now it was over, and he was back in the empty house
and counting the days till the office opened again. Even
Simon's company was preferable to his own, day after day.
Thank God he had his walking holiday booked for February.
Perhaps the Yorkshire moors would blow away his depression
and he could begin to pull himself together again. He could
only hope so.

'So – how was Christmas?'

They were sitting in a café in New Bond Street on a cold
January morning, with bags of sales purchases piled on the
chair between them.

Sophie shrugged. 'Pretty grim, as expected.'

'Did you tell him what you'd decided?'

'Not exactly; I just said I wanted to stay with Mum a bit
longer and we needed more time apart.'

'But not the "d" word?'

'No.'

Stella studied her over her coffee cup. 'Not having second thoughts, are you?'

'Oh, I don't know, Stella. He was really very sweet over Christmas, playing with Florence and being extra kind to Mum and me when we kept welling up. To be honest I felt a bit of a brute even saying we were staying on. He looked so . . . hurt.'

Stella was silent for a moment. Then she said, 'What about James?'

Sophie moved impatiently. 'James is James. Believe me, I'm under no illusions; even if I *do* divorce Mark, there'd be no chance of our marrying. In fact, I wouldn't want to. Imagine having to put up with his moods on a permanent basis!'

'But you are still seeing him, and – you know?'

'Yes, I'm still seeing him.'

'I miss our foursomes, now you're further away.'

'How are things with you and Lance?'

'Fine. Not as heavy as you two, though.'

'And Rex still doesn't suspect anything?'

She shook her head. 'But again, our relationship's different from yours and Mark's. Or at least, from how yours used to be. For example, our love life's pretty sporadic; I sometimes think he'd even be grateful to Lance for – filling in the gaps, as it were.'

Sophie gave a choke of laughter. 'You're incorrigible!' she said. She stirred her coffee reflectively. 'That reminds me, when we got back from Bournemouth Florence let slip Lance's name – said he'd bought her an ice cream or something. It was sheer bad luck, bumping into them like that after all our avoidance tactics. I tried to impress on her not to mention it, but—' She shrugged.

'So what happened?' Stella asked.

'Well, naturally Mark pounced on it, but I think I eventually convinced him he was *your* friend.'

'Which he is,' Stella pointed out.

'Though Mark might wonder if he'd brought someone along to partner me.'

'Did he ask?'

'No, he just accepted my word, as far as it went.'

Stella said shrewdly, 'You're feeling guilty, aren't you?'

'Of course I am. I always have.'

'But being with James is worth it?'

Sophie sighed. 'You make me sound so shallow. Sometimes I really hate myself.'

'Oh, come on, you're only young once and you've been positively saintly up to now. Enjoy yourself!'

But Sophie wasn't at all sure she was.

Clapham, London

Christmas had come and gone, studiously ignored at the Mallory house, and secretarial college had resumed. But as January slid remorselessly into February, whether at home, out with Tom or trying to master the exercises set for her, Ellie's mind kept returning to the postcard hidden in her drawer and the mysterious Douglas Crawford, until at last she could bear it no longer.

One evening, in the privacy of her room, she opened her laptop and logged on to the BT Phone Book. Then, holding her breath, she typed in his name and the address on the postcard. To her amazement, a telephone number immediately appeared. So he hadn't moved house in twenty years! She sat staring at it, mouth dry and heart pounding. Then, quickly, before she could change her mind, she dialled the number, her fingers trembling.

Across the miles she heard the ringing tone. Then it stopped and a man's voice said 'Douglas Crawford.'

Ellie froze, and he said again, a little impatiently, 'Hello? This is Douglas Crawford. Can I help you?'

She swallowed past the knot in her throat. 'Hello, yes – or at least I hope so. Could you tell me, please, if you once knew someone called Fay Mallory?'

There was a seemingly endless silence, then the connection was broken.

'Hello?' Ellie said futilely. Then, 'Damn, damn, damn!'

She immediately phoned Tom's mobile and before he had a chance to speak said rapidly, 'Tom, I've just spoken to him!'

'Hello to you too! What do you mean, who have you spoken to?'

'Douglas Crawford! Would you believe it, he's still at the same address and I looked up his phone number!'

'Oh my God!' Tom said slowly. 'What happened?'

'I asked if he knew Fay Mallory and he hung up on me.'

'There's your answer, then.'

'How do you mean?'

'Well, if he wasn't your father, the natural thing would have been to say, "Who's Fay Mallory?" or "Never heard of her." The fact that he didn't proves that he knew her.'

'So it does.' Ellie's heart was hammering. 'Well, he's not going to get off as easily as that.'

'What are you going to do?' Tom sounded anxious.

'Phone again in a day or two, but during office hours this time. Someone else might answer if he's at work, and perhaps I'd get more out of them.'

'Doesn't compute, Ellie. First, he's probably retired from work, and second, if he hasn't, it's extremely unlikely anyone else in that house will have heard of her.'

'Well, I'm going to try, anyway,' Ellie said stubbornly. 'And if that doesn't work, I'll go up to Cheshire and beard him in his den. It's half-term next week, so I'll tell Gran I'm going away with a friend.'

'Ellie, for God's sake stop this, before you get in any deeper! What possible good can come of it?'

'I owe it to Mum,' she said, and ended the call.

She waited a couple of days, then, in her lunch break, found a quiet corner and dialled the same number. This time it rang for longer but at last a woman's voice said tentatively, 'Hello?'

Ellie swallowed. 'Is that Mrs Crawford?' she asked, her voice shaking a little.

'No, love, you've just missed her. I'm the cleaner.'

'What time will she be back?'

'Oh, not for a while. They've all gone off on holiday.'

Ellie's eyes filled with tears of frustration, but a thought suddenly flashed into her head and she asked quickly, 'To Drumlee?'

'That's right, love. Perhaps you'd like to try again in about ten days? They should be back by then.'

Ellie thanked her and rang off. It was time to return to her desk, but an idea was already forming.

'You're off your chump!' Tom declared that evening.

'But don't you see, I've just got to know, once and for all. It's all right, I'm not going to demand any money or anything, I just want him to acknowledge Mum and me. And if he won't tell me on the phone, he'll have to do it face to face. So will you help me, like you promised?'

'Help you do what? You seem to be managing pretty well on your own.'

'Find a B and B in Drumlee.'

'You're mad! It'll be like the inside of a fridge up there at this time of year!'

'If he and his family can survive it, I can. I'll take warm clothes.'

'I wish I could come with you,' he said worriedly, 'but I can't take time off work.'

'I'll be OK. Let's have a look and see what's on offer.'

And it was as easy as that. The day before she was due to leave she made one last phone call, this time to the Merlin Hotel to make sure the Crawfords really were in Drumlee. She'd had to raid her savings for this trip – she couldn't risk it being in vain.

Safer, she thought, to ask for the wife, and when her call was answered she said brightly, 'Could you tell me, please, if Mrs Crawford is staying with you at the moment?'

'Not with us, no, madam; they're at their house, Touchstone. Have you that number?'

At which point Ellie's nerve failed her. 'Yes, thanks,' she lied rapidly. 'I'll try there. Thanks for your help.' And she rang off.

So her sitting duck was in position, and within the next few days she intended to have answers to all the questions that had troubled her throughout her life. Scotland, here I come! she thought triumphantly.

FOURTEEN

Drumlee

Sophie, then, not Florence. Mark drew a deep breath before scrolling rapidly through the missed calls in order to listen to them chronologically, conscious as he did so of the tingling in his ears and fingers as the cold began to bite. The morning was misty and, though no more snow had fallen, a thick white rime covered walls and gateposts.

The first message, sent about the time he'd switched off his phone on arrival here, was, as he might have expected, from Simon. Impatiently he skipped it and all Simon's subsequent ones, including the more surprising call from another office colleague, and urgently clicked on the earliest from the family, which came from Lydia and was dated last Sunday.

'Mark?' it began hesitantly. 'It's Lydia. I'm sorry to trouble you on holiday, but is Sophie with you, by any chance? No one seems to know where she is. Do please give me a call when you get this.'

His mother's first call had been made at ten o'clock on Monday. 'Mark, it's Mum. Why is your phone switched off? You've never done that before. How are we supposed to get in touch in an emergency? And as it happens this *is* one: Sophie seems to have disappeared, and we're wondering if by any chance she's with you? If so, it seems odd that she didn't tell anyone. Please give me a ring when you get this. Love from us all.'

Mark frowned. Why, in view of the state of their relationship, should anyone suppose she was with him? Hope that a reconciliation was on the cards, or the pressing need to know she was safe?

Safe. That word again; his mother had used it, and it increased his unease. Sophie could be thoughtless, but she wouldn't willingly cause Lydia concern. Margot's next two calls were indicative of increasing impatience at his inaccessibility and disquiet about Sophie, and by the last, the one he'd listened to first, anxiety had escalated to the point of calling in the police. What the hell was she playing at, worrying everyone like that?

He glanced back at the house. People would be gathering for breakfast and wondering where he was, but he had to find out what had happened. With luck, she might have turned up by now.

His call was answered on the first ring. 'Mark? Oh, thank God! *Is* she with you?'

'No, of course she's not, Mum. What the hell's going on?'

'Why did you switch – oh, never mind! The point is she told Lydia on Friday that she'd be spending the day and evening with Stella, and asked her to collect Florence from school. So Lyddie did so, gave her her tea, put her to bed and eventually went to bed herself. It wasn't till the next morning that she found Sophie's bed hadn't been slept in.'

'And there's been no word from her since?'

'None. Lydia got in touch with Stella, who confirmed that she'd seen her but said she'd thought Sophie went straight home. Though Lyddie thought she sounded a bit evasive.'

'Lance!' Mark said softly.

'What?'

'Florence mentioned they'd met someone called Lance in Bournemouth and Sophie told her not to tell me. When I tackled her about it, she said he was a friend of Stella's – but in that case, why the secrecy?'

'You mean she might be seeing someone?' Margot asked slowly.

'That's the likeliest explanation, though why she couldn't just have said so, I don't know. It's not as if we're still together. Ask Stella about him – she might know something.'

'How soon can you get back?'

Mark bit his lip. 'Mum, I can't. I'm . . . tied up at the moment. As long as Florence is OK – she is, isn't she?'

'Yes, of course – she thinks Sophie's on holiday. But what do you mean, you're tied up?' Her voice changed. '*You're* not with someone, are you?'

'Not in that sense. Look, I can't go into it now, and I'll

have to switch my phone off again. But I'll give you a call this evening, I promise.'

'Not in *what* sense?' she demanded. 'Why are you being so enigmatic?' And when he didn't reply, she ended, 'At least promise me you'll contact the police and let them know where you are and that you've not seen her.'

'Bye, Mum. Speak to you later.' He switched off his phone, slipped it into his pocket and hurried back to the house.

'Well, the wanderer returns!' Nick greeted him. 'One minute you were there, and the next you'd gone!'

'Sorry. Just needed a breath of fresh air.'

'It was more than fresh by the look of you!' Natalie handed him a cup of coffee. 'You look frozen!'

'That's very welcome, thanks.'

'Well, I hope you're over your hangover, if that's what it was,' Harry said, 'because we've got a guest for lunch, remember.'

'Guest?' Natalie repeated, then clapped a hand to her mouth. 'God, yes! With everything that's been going on, I'd completely forgotten! It's today Ellie's coming, isn't it?'

Sebastian frowned. 'Ellie? Oh, the girl who was on the bench.'

'Her mother died at Christmas, poor lamb, and apparently she loved Drumlee. That's why Ellie came.'

'She'd have done better to wait till summer,' Helena remarked. 'This weather's guaranteed to make her more, not less, miserable.'

'Then we must all try to cheer her up,' Natalie said firmly.

The kitchen radio, like all those at Touchstone, was tuned to the English rather than the Scottish news and Mark, gratefully sipping the hot coffee, was only half-listening when an item burst into his consciousness with the impact of a thunderclap.

'The condition of Victoria Pyne, the BBC presenter who was seriously injured in a car crash last week, continues to cause concern. Her husband Christopher, chief executive of the auction house Bellingham's, is at her bedside.'

Mark choked on his coffee, scalding his mouth in the process, and Jessica automatically patted his back. Last week . . . Simon's frantic calls . . . Oh God, no! He'd barely recovered his breath when the next item took it away again.

'Kent police are concerned for the safety of a thirty-two-year-old woman, Sophie Richmond, who disappeared from her mother's home in the village of Foxbridge last Friday. Anyone who might have seen her or who knows of her whereabouts is asked to get in touch with them on . . .' The requisite number was given. Then came the final shock. 'They're also anxious to trace her estranged husband, Mark Richmond, who is believed to be on a walking holiday in Yorkshire.'

'It's always the husband!' said Harry cheerfully.

Mark had tensed, awaiting immediate interrogation, before it struck him that the name would have no meaning here. Only Helena might have recognized it, and she'd doubtless forgotten it within minutes of being told.

Sure enough, to his enervating relief, everyone was calmly continuing with their breakfast, and he forced himself to relax.

'Egg and bacon, Adam?' Seb enquired from the cooker, and Mark, fervently blessing Adam Ryder, shook his head. 'I don't think I'll bother, thanks. Harry's right about the hangover, though. If you'll excuse me, I'll make myself scarce for a while and sort myself out in time for lunch.'

And pushing back his chair, he thankfully left the room.

Secure in the knowledge that Nick was in the kitchen, Mark ran upstairs, switching his phone on as he went, and, on reaching his bedroom, closed the door and scrolled back to Simon's first message. It was extremely brief.

'Phone me, Mark, for God's sake! All hell's broken out!'

Since he now knew the reason for his calls, Mark skimmed quickly through the others, all versions of the first with varying degrees of urgency. The call from Bob Derringer, one of the jewellery experts, was of more concern.

'It's Bob, Mark. Sorry to interrupt your leave, but you'll have heard by now of the boss's wife's accident – a very nasty one, I'm afraid. What's odd is that it was reported anonymously from a public call box, and the caller didn't wait to speak to the emergency services. Christopher's puzzled as to why she was even in that area, and as you were down there yourself that evening he wondered if you could shed any light on it.' He paused. 'Admittedly it's a long shot, since Simon says you spent the evening together and he's been unable to help. Anyway, give us a call when you get this message, and enjoy your leave.'

'Bloody Simon!' Mark said under his breath, and dialled his number.

'Mark! About bloody time! Hang on a minute.' There was the sound of footsteps and a door closing, then he came back on line. 'You've heard about Victoria?'

'Just now. How is she?'

'Still on the critical list.' His voice shook.

'What happened, Simon?'

'We were in her car, thank God, and she was driving. Sorry if that sounds callous, but if it had been mine I'd have been truly skewered.' He drew a breath. 'We'd been out for a meal and were on our way back to her hotel where I'd left my car when we came round a sharp corner, the wheels skidded and we went headlong into a tree.' His voice was shaking. 'The bonnet crumpled like cardboard and I could see that she was seriously hurt. We'd passed one of those old red phone boxes minutes before and I ran back and dialled nine-nine-nine.' He paused. 'You'll think me a heel for not using my mobile, but I couldn't risk it being traced.'

'So your call was anonymous,' Mark said flatly. The coward's way out – like his father, all over again.

'It didn't make any difference,' Simon blustered. 'The police and ambulance were there within minutes. I waited till I heard the sirens, then made my way back to the hotel. It was only a mile or so, but I've no idea how I got there. I was in total shock, frantic to know if she'd made it but with no way of finding out.'

His voice broke. Mark made no attempt to help him and after a minute he went on. 'I collected my car, hightailed it to our hotel and phoned you – and you bloody hung up on me. And you've been stalling me ever since.'

'I haven't been stalling you, Simon,' Mark said tiredly. 'My phone was switched off. I'm on holiday, remember.'

'Jenny said she rang,' he said after a minute. 'Thanks for playing along.'

'You do realize, don't you, that you've dragged me into

this? I've had a call from Bob Derringer saying among other things that you'd told them we'd spent the evening together.'

'Well, that's what we agreed, isn't it? And I'm very grateful that you stuck to it.'

'You'd better be,' Mark said grimly, 'because it's the last favour I'll ever do you. My career could be at risk if they find out I deliberately gave you a false alibi. Were you hurt yourself?' he added as an afterthought.

'Not a scratch. Ain't no justice, is there?' He hesitated. 'One thing's worrying me, though – apart from her injuries, I mean. If she's delirious or anything, she might . . . give something away.'

'You'll have to wait and see,' Mark said heartlessly. 'Goodbye, Simon. Please don't call me again.'

Bob Derringer, he decided, would have to wait a little longer for his return call.

He washed his face in cold water and patted it dry, surveying himself critically in the mirror over the basin. First Sophie, now Simon. Part of him acknowledged that he should return home; the other part demanded why the hell he should. If Sophie chose to go off with her lover, it was no business of his; Florence was OK, and that was all that really concerned him.

The family would be leaving Drumlee on Saturday, and if she still hadn't turned up, he supposed he could abandon his ill-fated walking holiday, for all the good it would do. On the other hand, ludicrous though it seemed, going home would lay him open to being seized by the police. And then there was Simon. God! And he'd thought his life was going off the rails before all this!

What he needed was space to sort himself out. He collected scarf and gloves from the shelf and ran back down the stairs, retrieving his windcheater from the banisters where he'd hung it on his way to breakfast. He was shrugging it on when a voice behind him said, 'And where are you sneaking off to?'

He turned to see Helena approaching from the kitchen. 'I'm hoping a stiff walk will dispel the hangover.'

'This convenient hangover again. Or is the truth that you find our company boring?'

'Don't be ridiculous, Helena,' he said shortly. He was in no mood for her games.

'Oh, so I'm being ridiculous, am I? Not very lover-like language, *caro mio*.'

'Not what you get from Blair Mackay?' he flashed back.

She drew in her breath sharply, then her hand lashed stingingly across his face. For a moment longer they stared at each other, both breathing heavily. Then he turned on his heel and let himself out of the front door. But not before he'd caught sight of Harry, Nick and Natalie, who'd also emerged from the kitchen and had witnessed the altercation.

Ellie arrived promptly at twelve thirty. She was wearing the familiar anorak and pink jumper, but the trainers had been changed for wedge-heeled shoes and the jeans for a long black skirt. Her hair, sleek and shiny, was caught back in a high ponytail, making her look even younger, Natalie thought.

'Come and get warm,' she invited, 'and meet the rest of the family.'

They awaited her in the sitting room in a slightly embarrassed group, and Natalie performed the introductions quickly, hoping to dispel the formal atmosphere. The girl seemed on edge, but who wouldn't be, faced with a room full of strange people?

'Is this your first visit to Drumlee?' Paula asked gently, as Seb, primed by Nick, handed Ellie a glass of shandy.

'Yes.' She gave a shy smile. 'I realize I'm not seeing it at its best, but Mum was always talking about it and I wanted to see it for myself.'

'We were so sorry to hear about your mother. How is your father coping?'

Damn! Natalie thought; her father's absence was an item she'd failed to pass on.

Ellie's hand had jerked involuntarily, spilling some of her drink, and she gave an exclamation of distress.

'Don't worry about it,' Paula said quickly. 'This carpet has had plenty of spills over the years. My sons assure me the alcohol preserves it!'

Ellie smiled uncertainly. 'I . . . never knew my father,' she said, reverting to Paula's question. 'Mum and I have always lived with my grandparents.'

Fortuitously Danny came to the rescue by slipping his hand in Paula's and announcing proudly, 'This is *my* granny!' and the tensions dissolved.

Since their guest was staying in a B&B, a substantial lunch had been planned. Meg and Andy had switched their services for the day from the evening to midday, producing a full-blown roast – Scottish beef with Yorkshire pudding, roast potatoes and two kinds of vegetable, followed by the queen of puddings. Their guest, however, seemed to have a disappointingly small appetite and Natalie worried that they'd over-faced her.

'Just eat as much as you want,' she urged.

'I'm sorry; it's delicious but I'm just . . . not very hungry.'

'Do you get a good evening meal at the B and B?' Douglas enquired.

It was the first remark he'd addressed directly to her, and she flushed. 'It's a kind of high tea,' she answered evasively.

'Kippers and bread and jam?' Harry asked, and she smilingly nodded.

This was not going as well as Natalie had hoped. 'I think you said you lived in London. So do I. Whereabouts are you?'

'Clapham,' Ellie replied.

'Really? I've friends who live there, on the edge of the Common.'

'Don't ask if she knows them!' put in Nick humorously. 'It's like being abroad; when you say you live in London, they ask if you know the Queen!'

Ellie pushed away her pudding plate and looked up. Her flush had intensified and her eyes were very bright. 'Actually,' she said, her voice unnaturally high, 'it isn't true, what I told you.' She took a deep breath. 'For a start, my mother never set foot in Drumlee in her life.'

They all stared at her, perplexed. 'Then what brought you here?' Paula asked after a moment.

'This.' Ellie opened the handbag on her lap and produced a picture postcard which she tossed on to the table. It was a view of Drumlee.

158

Anthea Fraser

'You just . . . liked the look of it?' Jessica suggested uncertainly.

'Not exactly. I wanted to meet you. I knew you were staying here, at a house called Touchstone, so I kept watch and when you came out, I . . . followed you.'

Her eyes fell before Natalie's accusing gaze. 'So our meeting wasn't just chance?'

Ellie shook her head.

'I'm afraid I don't understand,' Paula said quietly. '*Why* did you want to meet us, and why couldn't you have gone about it in a more orthodox way?'

Ellie squared her shoulders and looked directly at Douglas. 'Why did you hang up on me, Mr Crawford?' she asked.

Puzzled glances were exchanged, but Douglas was staring at the girl as though registering her for the first time. After an elongated pause he said in a strained voice, 'I'm sorry, I don't know what you're talking about.'

'I think you do. I asked if you knew Fay Mallory.'

'Who's Fay Mallory?' Paula demanded, alarmed at her husband's sudden pallor.

Ellie's eyes were still fixed on Douglas. 'My mother,' she said.

Someone gasped. Ellie leaned forward and retrieved the postcard. 'I found this at the back of a drawer when I was clearing out her things. It's from the Merlin Hotel, dated July 1999, and sent to Mr and Mrs Crawford in Knutsford, then forwarded to Mr Crawford in London. It reads: "Sorry to hear you won't be up this summer. Perhaps this card will change your mind?! Best – Lexie and Callum".'

Helena said under her breath, 'Oh my God!'

No one else spoke, so Ellie continued. 'My mother became pregnant, had a very difficult time, and nearly died giving birth to me. She was a semi-invalid for the rest of her life and – and died just before Christmas, as I said.' Tears were running unchecked down her cheeks.

Douglas said in a strangled voice, 'I didn't know!' Then he suddenly clutched his chest and fell forward across the table.

Ellie came to her feet, staring in consternation as everyone rushed to his aid and the two medics, Natalie and Nick, took charge. 'Phone for an ambulance!' Natalie instructed over her shoulder, and both her brothers fumbled for their phones.

Ellie was standing as though paralysed. She said in a choked voice, 'I never meant—'

'Then exactly what *did* you mean, you stupid little bitch?' Helena flung at her.

Ellie gave a sob and ran out of the room. Seconds later the front door slammed and they heard her footsteps running down the path.

Watching the frantic emergency measures in stunned disbelief, Mark wondered if the day could possibly get any worse.

FIFTEEN

Kent

Margot and Charles had tried to persuade Lydia to stay with them in Sophie's absence but she'd steadfastly refused on the grounds that her daughter might come back at any time to find an empty house. Feeling she and Florence shouldn't be alone, they'd therefore packed a case and temporarily moved to Dormers.

It had been a difficult and fraught few days, made worse by the fact that Florence was on half-term holiday and a constant pretence had to be maintained that all was well.

'Why hasn't Mummy phoned?' she'd asked more than once, and it was becoming increasingly difficult to think of satisfactory answers.

On the Wednesday morning, after a bad night followed by Mark's enigmatic phone call, the need to escape for a while began to build inside Margot and on an impulse she made some vague comment to Charles and Lydia, got into her car and drove the few miles home.

Since the central heating was on the twice-daily schedule the house felt cool and she didn't remove her coat. She made herself a cup of coffee and sat down with it at the kitchen table, trying to sort the chaos of her thoughts. She seemed already to have gone over every conceivable reason for Sophie's disappearance but none had been satisfying. Yes, the girl was often thoughtless and impulsive, but vanishing like this with no explanation was nothing short of cruel. After the shock of Peter's death, she wasn't sure how much more Lydia could stand.

Then there was Mark and his odd behaviour. He hadn't said where he was, nor why he was 'tied up', and had circumvented her demand to be more explicit. It was understandable that he'd lost patience with Sophie, but surely he was still concerned

for her welfare. She gave an exclamation of annoyance. Her
world seemed to be disintegrating about her.

Her eyes went round the familiar outlines of the room as
though seeking comfort from them. How many meals they'd
had at this table, she reflected, both formal and informal – with
Mark and Jon when they were young, later with Mark and
Sophie, then Jon and Delia, but consistently throughout all
those years with Peter and Lydia. When had been the last time
the four of them were here together? Not, despite repeated
invitations, since Peter's sixtieth birthday. Looking back, that
had been when things started to go wrong. If only she knew
why!

With the present so uncertain, it was a relief to let her mind
go back to happier times and her first meeting with the
Kingsleys. It had been shortly after she met Charles; they'd
been out together only a few times, to the theatre or dinner at
nearby restaurants, and when he phoned to say he'd like her
to meet his friends she'd been reluctant to share their date
with them. Peter and Lydia had been married just over a year,
and Charles introduced them as his best friend from university
and the first girl he'd fallen in love with – a comment that
had caused laughing protest.

'Don't listen to him, Margot!' Peter had reassured her. 'We
both met Lyddie on the same day and she and I were engaged
six weeks later. Charles was our best man.'

Whether or not due to Charles's tactlessness, though she'd
immediately liked Peter, who was handsome and charming
and thoroughly at his ease, she was less impressed with his
wife, whom she wrote off uncharitably as a dumb blonde.
Irritatingly pretty and well aware of it, she fluttered and flirted
like a butterfly, bestowing her dazzling smile on every man
within her orbit, be he waiter, cab driver or her husband's best
man.

It was some time before Margot began to see beneath the
façade to the warm and lovable person Lydia really was. In
the meantime she and Charles had married, and a few months
later she'd found she was pregnant. She'd broken the news to
Lydia when they were out on a foursome and the two men
had temporarily left them in search of drinks, and had been

totally unprepared for Lydia's reaction, which was to burst
into tears.

Alarmed, Margot had leaned across the table to take her
hand. 'Lydia, what is it? What have I said?'

Lydia, who cried as prettily as she did everything else,
hastily wiped her eyes. 'I'm so sorry,' she apologized. 'Of
course I'm delighted for you. When is it due?'

'If you're delighted, why the tears?' Margot asked gently.

They welled again. 'Because it's so unfair! You've only
been married five minutes, and Peter and I have been trying
for a baby for the last eighteen months. And what makes it
worse is that I've had a couple of misses.'

'Oh Lydia, I'm so sorry!' Margot exclaimed. 'I never gave
it a thought.'

'Of course you didn't, and I'm being silly and selfish as
usual. I'm sure it's just a question of time and all will be well.'

But Margot had given birth to two healthy sons before
Sophie, an adored ewe lamb, had put in an appearance. And
now that lamb had gone astray.

Lost in her memories, Margot found her coffee had grown
cold and stood up to put it in the microwave, watching
pensively as the pointer moved slowly to the time set. She
ought to get back, she thought. It was getting on for lunchtime, and since she'd taken over the cooking while they'd
been at Dormers, she doubted if Lydia would have made a
start on it. But oh, how she wished she and Charles were
back here, Sophie and Mark were together again, and all was
as it should be.

Overcoming her reluctance to return to Dormers and its
cloak of anxiety, Margot rinsed and dried her coffee mug and
replaced it in the cupboard. Then, determinedly fastening her
coat, she went back to her car.

Minutes later she turned into the Dormers driveway, parked
by the front door and, marshalling some cheerfulness from
deep inside her, went into the house.

'Hello?' she called. 'Anyone ready for lunch?'

There was silence except for the sound of a children's TV
programme upstairs.

'Hello?' she called again. 'Anyone home?'

She pushed open the sitting room door and stopped dead on the threshold. In the centre of the room Lydia stood sobbing in Charles's arms.

For a moment her heart stood still as a voice from the past echoed in her head: *This is the first girl I fell in love with!* Then they turned and, seeing her, simultaneously reached out, inviting her to join them, and the memory dissolved in a tide of love for them both as she went swiftly over to be enfolded in their embrace.

'For God's sake!' Lance burst out. 'If all you're going to do is moan about Sophie, I might as well go back to work!'

'I'm sorry, babe.' Stella reached up to touch his face. Now they were no longer in a foursome they'd reverted to meeting in Lance's flat in Pimlico. 'I'm really worried about her, though. It's not like her to go off like that without telling anyone – and she's certainly never left Florence before.' She hesitated. 'Are you sure James hasn't seen her?'

'He says not. Short of resorting to a lie detector, I have to accept that.'

'They were still seeing each other last month,' Stella said. 'So?'

'What did he actually say, when you asked him?'

Lance gave a dramatic sigh. 'I wasn't using a tape recorder.'

'Please, babe, just humour me?'

'That he hadn't seen her for a week or two. Look, you seem to be under the impression that we're bosom buddies. We're not. In fact, I only met him a couple of days before our first double date.'

'*What?*' Stella sat up and stared at him. '*Where* did you meet him, then?'

'In a pub. We got talking and he seemed pleasant enough. You'd suggested fixing Sophie up with someone, and since most of my friends were already spoken for I asked if he was game, and he said yes.' He hesitated. 'I admit that for a first date I thought he came on a bit strong in the car, but Sophie seemed to have no complaints.'

Stella was silent, mulling over this new perspective. 'So how many times have you actually met?'

'Well, we went down to Bournemouth together, but only to meet you two.'

'My *God*, so you know next to nothing about him?'

'I suppose not.' Lance looked uncomfortable. 'But come on, it's not that different from how you and I first got together, and she wouldn't have gone on seeing him if she hadn't been interested.'

Stella said slowly, 'I think at times he frightens her.' She frowned. 'Where does he live?'

'No idea, except it's a flat with a "deaf old biddy" living below him.'

'Then where does he work?'

'Don't know that, either.' He was sounding defensive now.

'Then how,' Stella asked with heavy patience, 'did you contact him to arrange the dates?'

'I have his mobile number, that's all.'

Stella frowned worriedly. 'We'd agreed to cover for each other, so when her mother rang on Sunday I said she'd been with me. But she's still not turned up and I'm getting really worried now, especially after what you've just said. Suppose I've hindered the search for her? I'm pretty sure Mrs Kingsley doesn't know about him.'

'Well, no. It's not the sort of thing you'd discuss with your mother. Especially if you're still married to someone else.'

'Perhaps I *should* tell her after all.'

'Tell her what, exactly? You don't even know for certain she was *with* James at the weekend – he told me she wasn't, remember – let alone where he lives. And if Sophie's mum starts digging it might lead back to us; then your husband could get wind of it.'

'I wish you'd told me, that's all.'

'Told you what?' He was beginning to lose patience.

'That he was such an unknown quantity. I feel responsible for her, having talked her into meeting him in the first place.'

'Well, you didn't twist her arm; she must have been up for it.'

'You've got his mobile number,' Stella said suddenly. 'Ring him now!'

'Now?'

'Why not? He'll be on his lunch break from wherever it is he works.' And, as he hesitated, 'Please, Lance.'

Grumbling, he reached for the chair where he'd tossed his jacket, retrieved his mobile and, muttering under his breath, tapped in the number. After a few minutes it went to voicemail.

'Great!' said Stella heavily.

'Look, I'll try again later, OK? Now for God's sake lie down and let's get on with what we came here for. Time's ticking, you know, and I'm already taking an extended lunch hour.'

Stella ran her hand distractedly through her hair but he reached up, tugged gently on her wrist and pulled her down to him, and with a sigh she put Sophie out of her mind.

Miss Elise Philpott, ex-headmistress and Justice of the Peace, looked up from her newspaper and frowned. There it was again, that muffled sound that she couldn't quite identify, coming from the flat above. But it was midday and the young man (she couldn't remember his name – if, indeed, she'd ever heard it) had left for work as usual that morning. The front door had slammed while she was having her breakfast.

Could it be rats? She gave a shiver. Perhaps she should contact the landlord, but surely that was up to the occupier? Maybe a word with him, then, in the first instance. They'd not exchanged more than a couple of words when he first moved in – a rather brusque young man, she'd thought, and although he'd been civil enough she hadn't felt entirely comfortable with him, a feeling exacerbated last Friday when he'd brought a girl back with him, strictly against tenancy rules.

She'd been opening her bedroom window when his car drew up, and she'd noticed with disapproval that he'd had to support his companion into the house. Drunk, she supposed, thinking nostalgically of all the young girls she'd nurtured over a lifetime of teaching, when discipline and self-respect had to a large extent forestalled such behaviour. Times had certainly changed, she thought regretfully, and not for the better.

Such a shame old Mr Baines had died; he'd been an ideal neighbour, and they'd occasionally enjoyed a game of cribbage in the evenings. Too bad, she thought with a self-deprecating smile, that she wasn't consulted on the conviviality or otherwise of her neighbours!

Another indistinct sound from above – could it be described as a squeak? This really wasn't good enough; she'd waylay her neighbour on his return this evening and have a word. She picked up her paper again, but was again interrupted, this time by the telephone.

'Hello, Aunt!'

'Colin!' It was her favourite nephew and her heart lifted. 'How nice to hear from you.'

'Just to say I'll be in your area tomorrow, and am hoping you'll have lunch with me.'

'How kind – I should be delighted.'

'Excellent! It's some time since I saw you. How are you?'

'I'm well in myself, thank you, but unfortunately I'm having a slight problem with the flat at the moment, which is causing me some worry.'

'What kind of problem?'

She hesitated. 'This sounds fanciful, but I keep hearing noises from the flat above me after the tenant has left for work. I thought at first it was my imagination, but now I'm wondering if it could be rats.'

'Good grief! How long has this been going on?'

'I've only noticed it this last week. It's probably nothing, but I'm continually on edge, listening for it.'

'Well, we can't have that. When I collect you tomorrow, I'll see if I can suss out what's causing it. In the meantime, try not to worry. I'm sure we'll get to the bottom of it.'

'That would be such a relief, dear,' she said gratefully.

'Still no news?'

Jonathan had barely closed the front door behind him. 'Yes and no,' he said, dropping his briefcase on the floor. 'Mum's finally established contact with Mark.'

'But Sophie's not with him?'

'No, but then we never really thought she was.'

'Could he offer any suggestions as to where she might be?'

He shook his head. 'In fact, old Mark was being a bit cagey.

Said he was "tied up" at the moment and couldn't come home, and – the really odd thing – he turned off his mobile again, promising to phone Mum this evening.'

Delia frowned. 'Why ever would he do that?'

Jonathan shrugged. 'Search me, unless he's got some woman holed up there. I could use a drink.' He walked past her into the sitting room. 'G and T?'

She nodded, slowly following him and perching on the arm of a chair, her arms wrapped round her as though she were cold.

'You do think she's – all right – don't you?'

'Sophie? God knows. I suppose she must have had some sort of meltdown.'

Delia shuddered as she took her glass from him, and he frowned.

'Are you OK, love? I didn't think there was much love lost between the two of you.'

'That doesn't mean I want anything to happen to her.' She took a quick drink, grimacing as the coldness of it numbed her throat. She looked up at his concerned face. 'You don't think she might have done anything silly, do you? She was very close to Peter, and her marriage is in the process of breaking down. She's not in a good place at the moment. Suppose she decided to . . . follow his example?' Her voice shook. 'Then I'd have that on my conscience as well.'

'Good God, darling,' Jonathan exclaimed, 'you can't think like that!' Removing her glass, he pulled her to her feet and into his arms, where she clung to him, her nails digging into his shoulder. 'Sophie might be a scatterbrain like her mother, bless her, but she's got her head screwed on. There's no way she'd do anything like that.'

'Then where *is* she, Jonathan?'

'I wish I knew,' he said.

Jenny Lester came slowly downstairs after settling her children and stood in the sitting room doorway surveying her husband. He was sitting forward on his chair, holding a whisky glass between his knees and staring down into it.

Bracing herself, she came into the room and sat down

opposite him. 'Are you going to tell me what's wrong?' she asked quietly.

His head jerked up and it took a moment for his eyes to focus. 'Work,' he said after a pause.

She shook her head. 'Sorry. Not good enough.'

He made to take a drink, saw that his glass was empty and set it down on the coffee table.

'You're having an affair, aren't you?'

His head shot up again, his lips framed in a denial. Then his face crumpled, he covered it with his hands and began to weep, great sobs racking his body. She sat motionless, watching him, as the minutes ticked by. Eventually the paroxysm lessened and, with a shuddering gulp, stopped. He wiped his face with his hands, then fished in his trouser pocket for a handkerchief and blew his nose. Finally he looked up, meeting her steady gaze.

'How long have you known?' he asked in a low voice.

She shrugged. 'Weeks? Months? And I'd be surprised if this is the first.'

His eyes filled again and he swallowed convulsively. 'Why didn't you say anything?'

'Because I didn't want to rock the boat while the children are so young.'

He gazed at her with wet, reddened eyes. 'Then why now?'

'Because this time it's different and I can't go on pretending nothing's wrong.'

He said flatly, 'I really thought I loved her.'

'No doubt,' she answered expressionlessly. 'And do you "really think" you love me?'

He flinched. 'I *know* I do,' he said.

'Then why, Simon?'

After a beat, he said in a low voice, 'Because I'm a bloody fool and I don't deserve you.'

'I agree on both counts.'

There was a long silence while the gas fire popped and the clock ticked. Then he said quietly, 'Are you going to leave me?'

'If there's any leaving to be done, you'll be the one doing it. The children and I are staying put, in our home.'

He shook his head wonderingly, 'How can you be so calm?'

'Because I've had plenty of time to think about it.'

Hardly daring, he asked, 'Do you still love me?'

'To be honest, I don't know. Certainly not at this precise moment, and if you want to stay it'll be under strict conditions. In the meantime I've moved your things into the guest room.'

His eyes widened. 'For how long?'

'That's up to you.'

After a while he nodded agreement. 'Thank you,' he said humbly.

By that evening, Stella was unable to quieten her conscience any longer. While Rex was engrossed in the television she went into the kitchen, shut the door and, steeling herself, took out her phone.

'Mrs Kingsley? It's Stella.'

'You've heard from Sophie?' Vibrant hope rang in her voice.

'I'm afraid not.' She paused, then added with difficulty, 'And what's more, I have to tell you I wasn't being truthful last time we spoke. I didn't see her on Friday.'

She heard Lydia's indrawn breath. 'Then why say that you had?'

This was even more difficult. 'The truth is we've occasionally been out in a foursome and we'd agreed to . . . cover for each other.'

'A foursome? You mean – not with your husbands?'

'No; I'd met someone and had a few drinks with him, and Sophie was feeling bored so I asked him to bring along a friend for her.'

There was a silence while Lydia absorbed this. Then she said, 'But if you were a foursome . . .?'

'Well, yes, that's how it started. But since Sophie's been down with you we've lost touch a bit, and I think she was continuing to meet James on her own.'

'Oh my God!' Lydia breathed. 'Then who *is* this James? And surely, when I phoned, you got in touch with him?'

Stella took a deep breath. 'Lance – the man I'm seeing – did, and he said he hadn't seen her. I'd thought he and Lance were friends, but I found out today that they'd met only recently, and Lance doesn't know where he lives or works or, in fact, anything about him. He *said* his surname was Meredith, but . . .'

'It might not be,' Lydia said starkly.

'I'm beginning to wonder. His phone went to voicemail today, and when I checked directories online, I couldn't find any entry for him.'

'And you've no idea at all where he lives?'

'No, except that he told Lance there's a deaf old lady in the flat below.'

'Very helpful,' said Lydia.

Stella's voice broke. 'Oh, Mrs Kingsley, I'm so terribly sorry! If anything's happened to her—'

'So in essence you're telling me we've wasted nearly a week; she could be anywhere, with God knows who, and we've no means whatever of tracing her.' Her voice hardened. 'Is there anything else you're not telling me?'

'No, that's all, I promise.'

'Thank you for calling, then,' said Lydia Kingsley, and hung up.

Stella sat down at the table, put her head in her hands and burst into tears.

Miss Philpott spent an uneasy night. She'd heard her fellow tenant return as usual at about seven and considered going into the hall to intercept him, but refrained. She'd wait till she'd seen Colin; there might be a simple explanation and she didn't want to appear an interfering old fool.

Although there were the odd thumps during the evening and an occasional snatch of sound from a television programme, there was nothing she could attribute to rats – but then they'd hardly appear when someone was in the flat, so that was no comfort.

She was waiting with her hat and coat on when Colin arrived just after noon the following day.

'All quiet on the home front?' he enquired with a grin, kissing her cheek.

'At the moment, yes.'

'You really are sure you heard something? I mean, it couldn't just have been coming from outside, or anything?'

'My dear boy, I might have had to resort to glasses in my sixties, but there's nothing wrong with my hearing, which is excellent.'

He glanced a little apprehensively up the staircase ahead of them. 'And you're sure the tenant has gone out?'

'Of course. I watched him drive away.'

'Very well, then; let's see what we can find – holes in the wainscoting, for instance.'

They went together up the stairs and stood on the landing, looking at the closed door ahead of them.

'Perhaps if we make a noise it might startle them into giving themselves away,' Colin suggested and, taking hold of the door knob, he shook it vigorously. Immediately there was a scuffling sound from inside the room.

'There!' Miss Philpott exclaimed triumphantly. 'Rattle it again!'

He did so, putting his ear against the wood of the door. 'There are certainly noises,' he said slowly as he straightened, 'but it doesn't sound like rats to me.'

He put his mouth to the gap between door and frame. 'Hello?' he called. 'Is anyone there?'

Miss Philpott stared at him in astonishment, but to her amazement a decided scrabbling sound reached them, followed by a slight bump and an almost inaudible whimpering sound.

'My God,' Colin said slowly, 'there *is* someone in there!'

Miss Philpott swallowed convulsively. 'But who—?' She broke off, clutching her nephew's arm. 'He brought a young woman back with him last week,' she said rapidly. 'I assumed she was drunk – he was virtually holding her up. And now that I think of it, I never actually saw her leave.'

They looked at each other, assessing a totally new possibility. 'But *would* you have seen her leave?' he asked.

'Not necessarily, no, but it's possible she could still be here.'

'Then why didn't she answer when I called?'

'Well, it's against the rules for her to be here.'

He shook his head. 'I may be reading too much into it, but it sounded to me as though whoever it is – *if* there's anyone and it's not just rats – is in some kind of distress. But whether it's rats or human, we should get in touch with the landlord straight away. He'll have keys to the flat and can check it out. Have you got his number?'

'Yes, in my phone book.' She turned to go back downstairs.

Colin put his mouth to the door again. 'Don't worry,' he said, 'we're going to get help.' He paused. 'Can you make a noise if you can hear me?'

There was a soft but unmistakable thump and he let out his breath in a soundless whistle.

'Hang on,' he called, 'we won't be long.' And he ran down the stairs after his aunt.

SIXTEEN

Drumlee

I t had been a surreal afternoon. Paula had accompanied
Douglas in the ambulance, but with the paramedics still
working on him there'd been no room for Nick and Natalie,
who reluctantly rejoined the others in the sitting room while
the caterers, pale with shock, hovered in the background,
waiting for the opportunity to clear the dining room.

Mark's instinct as an outsider was to make himself scarce.
Although Nick was in a similar position, he had at least helped
in the emergency and was now discussing with Natalie the
most likely outcome, and it occurred to Mark that he should
first make his peace with Helena.

'She's gone out,' Harry said, when asked if he'd seen her.
'Didn't she tell you?'

'I'll see if I can catch her up,' Mark replied, aware that
Harry had seen the earlier altercation. Not that he'd any real
desire to see her, but they'd have to patch up their silly tiff if
they were supposed to be engaged. He was rapidly running
out of patience with her.

Once more he let himself out of the house but, abandoning
any plan to look for Helena, turned away from the town and
started walking steadily uphill, following the road as it curved
round towards the coast while his thoughts processed the events
of the last few hours.

Douglas's collapse had temporarily blotted out Ellie's
bombshell but it was lurking under the surface and, with him
out of the way, the family would be free to discuss its impli-
cations. *Don't think it's always been a bed of roses*, Helena
had told him that first day, when discussing her parents'
marriage. How would Paula react, once the immediate
urgency abated? And what of the girl herself? She'd looked
stricken when Douglas collapsed, and Helena's vindictive

taunt wouldn't have helped. What had been her motive in searching out her father after all these years? If indeed he *was* her father, but after his reaction there didn't seem much doubt. Was money her object, or simply recognition? There was no way of knowing, but from any angle it sounded a tragic story.

Moving from one crisis to another, his thoughts turned to Sophie and her uncharacteristic disappearance. What the hell was she playing at? Was she trying to get back at him in some way, or was he just being paranoid? He didn't see why he should cut short a much-needed break to dance attendance on her. Yet that word 'safe' continued to disturb him.

Women! he thought. A plague on both their houses!

It was getting dark by the time Mark returned to Touchstone, and as he closed the gate behind him a flake of snow brushed against his face. Certainly time to be indoors.

The family was having tea in the sitting room and Natalie, greeting him with a smile, poured him a cup.

'Any news?' he asked, moving to the fire to get warm.

'Mum phoned an hour ago. It's not as serious as it seemed, thank God. He might be allowed out tomorrow, but he won't be fit to drive home on Saturday, so they'll stay on for another week.'

'Hope they don't get snowed in,' Mark commented. 'It's starting to fall again.'

The phone rang in the hall and Natalie, who was nearest the door, hurried to answer it and, assuming it would be news from the hospital, switched to speaker as she returned.

'Hello?' she said. 'Mum?'

But the call was not from the hospital. 'No, it's Lexie. Is that Natalie? Look, I don't want to trouble your mother, but could you pass on a message when you next speak to her? She asked me to ring round any B and Bs open this time of year and to ask for a girl called Ellie. I managed to track her down, and it took some persuasion but she finally agreed to stay on till Paula can speak to her.'

The family exchanged glances. 'Thanks, Lexie, we'll tell her.'

'I gather your father's over the worst?'

'Yes, with luck he'll be out tomorrow; but they'll stay on at least a week while he recovers.'

'Well, that's good news.' She paused. 'Could I have a word with Helena, please?'

Natalie glanced round the room. 'Where *is* Hellie?'

'Probably upstairs,' Harry suggested. 'I presume she came back with you, Adam?'

Mark looked startled. 'Me? No, I haven't seen her.'

'But you said you'd catch her up?'

'Yes, but I realized she had a head start, and since I'd no idea which direction she'd taken I gave up and just went for a walk.'

'Then has *anyone* seen her?' Sebastian demanded.

'She went out straight after lunch,' Jessica offered.

Lunch! It seemed an eternity since that meal in the dining room – Ellie's dramatic announcement and Douglas's even more dramatic collapse.

'Did she take the car?' pressed Sebastian.

Jessica shook her head. 'I was watching the ambulance leave, and saw her run out of the gate.'

Lexie's voice cut in, suddenly sharp with anxiety. 'Isn't she there?'

'She doesn't seem to be,' Natalie replied. 'Perhaps she's at the hospital.'

'She wasn't when I spoke to Paula half an hour ago.'

'Then she *must* be in our room. I'll get her.'

Barely a minute later she was back, growing alarm on her face. 'No sign of her!' she said.

'Then where the hell is she?' Sebastian asked.

Lexie's voice again, sounding increasingly urgent. 'Have you found her?'

'No,' Harry replied. 'No one seems to have seen her since lunch.'

'Then could you try her mobile?'

Natalie said sharply, 'Is something wrong?'

'Just try it, please. I'll explain later.'

Frowning, Natalie extracted her own mobile from her handbag and clicked on her sister's number. After a couple of rings a voice announced, 'The number you are trying to contact is currently unavailable. Please try again later.'

'Did you hear that?'

'Yes,' Lexie replied bleakly.

'It probably only means she's forgotten to charge it.'

'Nevertheless, I have to speak to you. I'll be with you in ten minutes.' And she rang off.

They looked at each other in bewilderment. 'What's that all about?'

'Are you sure you haven't seen her, Adam?' Harry asked.

'For God's sake!' Mark broke out. 'I've said so, haven't I?'

Sebastian raised a hand. 'All right, everyone, keep calm. Let's see what Lexie has to say. It must be important, if she's coming round hotfoot.'

They'd not long to wait. It seemed the phone call had barely ended when the doorbell rang and Lexie, white-faced and with snowflakes in her hair, was being ushered into the room and installed in a chair beside the fire. She looked round quickly.

'She's still not back, then?'

'As you see,' Sebastian answered. 'What's this about, Lexie?'

She drew a deep breath, her hands laced tightly together. 'There's something I have to tell you. God knows I don't want to, but it might be important. The point is, she came to the hotel this afternoon.'

'Helena did? Well then, surely . . .'

Lexie shook her head. 'She and Blair had a blazing row and she stormed out in a highly volatile state. Of course, we assumed she'd come straight back here, but when I phoned and you said—' She broke off, running a hand over her face.

'I'm breaking confidences and I hate to do it, but in the circumstances I've no option if you're to understand why we're so concerned.' She took a deep breath. 'You know that Helena and Blair had a boy and girl thing going when they were young, and it continued to some extent each year as a light-hearted holiday romance.' She flicked a glance at Mark, then away. 'Until, that is, a couple of summers ago, when it took a more serious turn. Blair has always been fond of her but accepted long ago that she regarded it as just a harmless flirtation. Then, during the previous winter, he'd finally put past hopes behind him and fallen in love with a local girl.'

She tipped her head back suddenly, eyes closed. 'Have you *any idea* how much I hate this?'

No one answered her, just waited for her to continue. After a minute she did so. 'Then, of course, that summer arrived and you all came back.' She sighed. 'I love Helena dearly, but, well, she was jealous, I suppose. Whatever the reason, she went after him with no holds barred, and his defences crumpled.'

'I don't remember this,' Harry broke in, frowning.

'It was the summer she had extended leave following glandular fever, and she stayed on after the rest of you went home. And the long and the short of it was that Blair became besotted with her and ended it with Kirsty, breaking her heart in the process.'

Sebastian moved impatiently. 'I'm sorry, but this is all history. If she's really missing, we should be out looking for her.'

'Don't worry, there's a search going on, but please bear with me for another minute – it's very relevant. Well, as I was saying they spent every available minute together, but when Blair wanted to announce their engagement she stalled, saying she must tell her parents first, which, of course, was fair enough. So she went back to London, and the following week a brief note arrived saying it had been fun but she hadn't meant him to take it so seriously and she'd now met someone else.'

There were tears in Lexie's eyes. 'He was stunned,' she continued. 'He realized, to put it bluntly, that he'd been played for a fool and lost Kirsty in the process – she'd taken a job in France in an attempt to put it all behind her.'

Lexie straightened her shoulders, glancing at their concerned faces. 'Last year, if you remember, Helena didn't come up with you – she was off sailing with her boyfriend, we were told – so this is the first time they've met since. Blair's still very bitter, but for old times' sake and because he's fond of you all, he was determined not to show it. And this week, unbelievably, she – she tried to revive it.'

And here she looked at Mark for a long minute. 'He pretended not to notice,' she went on, 'but this afternoon after your father'd been taken to hospital, she turned up at the hotel in a very distressed state and practically threw herself into his arms. He comforted her as best he could, but when she tried to – to kiss him, he held her off and made some laughing comment about her being an engaged woman. And – oh God!' She put a hand to her mouth.

Mark had stiffened, coldness seeping down his spine as he saw the direction this was taking.

'And that's when she told him,' Lexie continued unsteadily, 'that her so-called engagement was just a charade to pre-empt Natalie's, and that she now realized he was the one she wanted.'

Everyone looked at Mark. When he didn't speak, she went on, 'She even said Adam Ryder isn't his real name – it was one she'd made up weeks ago – and she only met him the day you all came up here.'

Into the silence Sebastian demanded harshly, 'Is this true?'

Mark swallowed and straightened his shoulders. 'Yes, it is. I was going on a walking holiday, and at the station she mistook me for an escort she'd booked.'

'*Escort?*' Sebastian interrupted sharply.

Natalie made a dismissive gesture. 'There's a firm she uses when she needs a partner for official dinners. She told me about it – it's all quite above board.'

Attention switched back to Mark, and he continued. 'Well, she wouldn't let me explain and virtually manhandled me on to the train.' He shrugged. 'I'd nothing to lose, so I agreed to play along.'

'My God!' said Nick softly. Then, 'So what *is* your name?'

'Mark Richmond.'

Harry looked up suddenly. 'Mark—? Isn't that the guy in the news whose wife is missing?' His eyes narrowed. 'And now – surprise, surprise – so is Helena!'

'Harry!' Sebastian said sharply. 'That's quite enough!' He turned to Lexie. 'You'd better finish what you came to say.'

She passed a hand over her face. 'That was the point when Blair finally snapped. All the hurt came pouring out and he accused her of playing fast and loose with everyone's feelings and ruining his chances of a happy marriage with Kirsty. He finished by saying he never wanted to see her again.' She bit her lip. 'He told me she looked traumatized and he immediately wanted to take at least some of it back. But she spun round and fled, and he didn't try to stop her.'

After a minute Natalie asked, 'What time was that?'

Lexie shrugged. 'About three, I suppose.'

Harry had come to his feet. 'And it's now after six.' He again looked at Mark, his eyes still suspicious. 'You didn't get back till around five. Are you sure you didn't go after her?'

Lexie said quickly, 'When I phoned you about the girl and Hellie wasn't here or answering her mobile, Callum and Blair immediately organized a search party. They're out looking for her now.'

'But it's dark!' Natalie exclaimed, her voice rising. She glanced at the uncurtained window. 'And it's snowing quite heavily. Suppose she's lying hurt somewhere? She wouldn't survive the night in this weather.'

'We'll go and join them,' Sebastian said, turning sharply as a little voice from the doorway asked plaintively, 'Is it nearly teatime?'

Natalie, pale-faced, came to her feet. 'Yes, darling, it certainly is,' she replied, going to her nephew and taking his hand. 'And you can choose what you'd like to have. Let's go and look in the fridge.'

The rest of them had also stood. Lexie said softly, 'I'm so very sorry about this.'

'Hardly your fault – or Blair's,' Sebastian said briskly. 'Provided Helena's OK, let's hope it's taught her a lesson. Right, everyone, wrap up – boots, if we have them. It'll be pretty unpleasant out there.'

Mark said quietly, 'I'd like to come with you, if I may.'

Harry made a movement of protest, but Seb said firmly, 'Of course, the more the better.'

Joining the general movement towards the door, Nick gave Mark a very welcome grin of sympathy. 'Reckon you got more than you bargained for!' he said in a low voice.

*   *   *

It was the longest evening any of them could remember. It had been agreed that news of Helena's absence should be kept from Paula, and that Natalie would stall should her mother phone and ask to speak to either of her brothers.

The Touchstone part of the search had meanwhile split into two. Mark and Nick volunteered to cover the area between the house and hotel, while the Crawfords, who'd established mobile contact with Blair, went back in the car with Lexie to help search the town centre and the front. Snow was falling heavily, reducing visibility to a few feet and stinging their faces with splinters of ice, while the wind, fiercely bitter, penetrated their clothes and numbed their ears.

Mark, head down and gripping one of the torches Sebastian had supplied, wondered uneasily if his dig about Blair Mackay that morning had sent Helena hotfoot into his arms. He could only hope not. It was ironic that he'd left Chislehurst hoping for a respite from his worries, and had ended up suspected of involvement in the disappearance of two women.

He sent up an incoherent prayer that they'd both soon be found safe and well.

An hour later he and Nick had combed the road down into town, together with several of the side streets, inch by inch, calling Helena's name every so often. They'd met no one on their travels – hardly surprising, given the weather. Almost stiff with cold, buffeted by the increasingly strong wind, they had paused in the shelter of a hedge to take stock. Neither of them liked to be the first to suggest returning to the house, but both felt they'd exhausted every possibility of Helena's being in the vicinity. Then, above the howl of the wind, came the reassuringly familiar sound of a mobile.

Nick scrabbled frantically in the pocket of his greatcoat, his fingers almost too numb to open it. 'Yes?' he said breathlessly.

'We've got her!' It was Harry's jubilant voice.

'That's great! Is she OK?'

'Hypothermic and with a badly sprained ankle, but alive, thank God. We're dropping her off at the hospital and will take the opportunity to pop in to see the parents, but we'll be back at the house in about an hour. All details then.'

He rang off. Nick fumbled the phone back into his pocket and he and Mark exchanged an instinctive hug of relief before thankfully setting off back up the hill.

It was after nine o'clock when Blair dropped Seb and Harry back at the house, declining their invitation to go in. 'We'll touch base again tomorrow,' he said.

Seated round the fire as they thawed out, whisky macs in hand, they recounted how they'd liaised with the group from the hotel, comprising Callum, Blair, Jean-Luc and a couple of waiters. It had been one of the latter who'd found her, huddled on a bench a fair way along the promenade. She'd been too weak to question, but it seemed clear that having fled the hotel in a turbulent state of mind, she'd felt the need to calm down before returning home, and set off along the promenade hoping the icy air would restore some sense of balance. It wasn't, of course, snowing at the time.

At some stage she must have slipped on a patch of ice, sprained her ankle and found it impossible to put it to the ground. The final straw would have come when she realized her mobile had run out of battery.

'Anyway,' Seb concluded, sipping his drink appreciatively, 'she was coming round by the time we left, so she should also be home tomorrow. When, incidentally, she'll have quite a bit of explaining to do, including an apology to Adam-stroke-Mark for getting him into this mess.'

Harry glanced at Mark shamefacedly. 'And I owe you one, too,' he said gruffly. 'Put it down to the heat of the moment, but I'm sorry I talked out of the back of my head.'

Mark nodded acceptance and Seb added, 'And talking of apologies, it seems there's another forthcoming. Dad and Mum have obviously had a long talk, and the upshot is that they've invited Ellie to come back later in the week, so we can get to know her properly.'

'So she *is* his daughter!' breathed Natalie.

'It seems so, though to give him his due, he only found out today.'

Having been too caught up in events to phone home the previous evening, Mark was determined to repeat his early morning call of the day before and, this time wrapped more warmly, he again went down before breakfast and let himself out of the house, his footsteps crunching in the fresh snow, and took up his position beyond the screening hedge.

As before, his call was answered on the first ring. 'Mark! You promised to ring last night!'

'I know, Mum, but all kinds of things blew up—'

'Here too,' she interrupted, 'but the main thing is we've found Sophie!'

He let out his breath in a long sigh, watching it vaporize in the cold air. 'Thank God for that. And what was her excuse?'

His mother's tone was grave. 'She'd a very good one, Mark. She'd been kidnapped, would you believe, kept tied up, gagged and sedated.' Margot's voice faltered.

Mark stiffened disbelievingly. '*What?*'

'Apparently she and Stella had been seeing a couple of men – Lydia swears she had no idea – and one of them turned decidedly nasty. Anyway, an old lady became suspicious after hearing odd noises in the flat above, and she and her nephew found her.' She gave a brief laugh. 'Lyddie said the man told Stella's boyfriend his neighbour in the flat below was deaf. Well, she might have looked frail but she'd the hearing of a bat, and that was his undoing. The police were waiting for him when he returned last night.'

'But how's Sophie now? And *where* is she?'

'In Sevenoaks Hospital, very shaken, badly bruised and traumatized, as you'd expect.' Her voice changed. 'Darling, I know you've had your differences and she's behaved foolishly, but this experience has made her finally grow up. She – she keeps asking for you.'

In that snow-covered Scottish street Mark stood immobile, his mind baulking at the vision his mother had conjured up of his lovely Sophie with her face battered and bruised. How *dared* that bastard treat her like that? A wealth of feelings, previously suppressed, surged inside him, an amalgam of anger and overwhelming protective love. Sophie and little Florence: they were his world. What the hell was he doing up here, hundreds of miles away?

'Mark?' Margot said tentatively.

'It'll be OK, Mum,' he said. 'I'm coming home.'